NOVEMBER FROST

BOOK 2 OF THE FROST WITCH SAGA

BONNIE ELIZABETH

COURTNEY

ourtney knew she looked beyond haggard. The sleepless nights left bags beneath her eyes so large and dark that even if she dressed up in clown makeup they'd show through. She felt every bit of the fatigue that drew her lower lids halfway down to her chin.

Outside the billing office, she heard the sounds of patients and nurses talking, phones ringing, a dull white noise that didn't help keep her awake, particularly as the clinic was slow. People in Central Kentucky didn't like to drive in the snow.

It was barely mid-November and they'd had more snow than northern Canada. You'd think people would learn to handle the roads. The soft fire of the irritation woke Courtney enough to listen to Wendy, the assistant office manager, calling for attention.

"We're heading out," Wendy said. "All admin staff get to go home and expect to be off for several days. There's no break in the storm this time." Wendy sounded excited to be the one delivering the news. Courtney didn't care that much. What did she have to go home to?

The black office chair squeaked as Courtney stood. She bent to get her umbrella, something she'd taken to carrying. Her problems had started back in October when she'd gone out into the snow without covering her head. Some instinct suggested the lack of covering was the reason she was suffering now. Not from a cold or pneumonia, but from the terrors of a creature that called her name throughout the night and sometimes told her to kill people.

Courtney reached the coat closet first and grabbed her ski jacket. Usually, that was all she needed to stay warm. Lately, she'd been thinking she needed something warmer and when her brain was functional enough she took to pouring over LL Bean catalogs online.

It was something to do in the middle of the night when the house called her name.

Courtney had tried earplugs, which didn't work. She still heard her name being called. She tried using her earbuds and blocking out the sounds with music, but the voices interrupted the songs, singing her name at the most awkward times.

She'd gotten so desperate that one night, about a week ago, she'd called her friend Hannah to come over and spend the night. The voices were silent then. Nothing. No laughter. No written notes. Courtney felt rested for the first time in ages.

When Hannah left, and Courtney had put some clothes in the washer, her computer had started chanting, "Kill Hannah. Kill Hannah," in a robotic voice.

The worst part of the chant was that Courtney felt like she wanted to kill Hannah. She wanted to feel her friend's throat beneath her fingers, perhaps feel the silk of her hair as she ripped it from her head, watch as the light disappeared from her eyes. Courtney would drink in the warming terror of Hannah's last moments and be sated, at least for a few days.

The thoughts came from nowhere and everywhere. They made Courtney's stomach twist in knots and bile rise in her throat.

Her insanity, if that's what it was, began with the first snow and worsened every time the snow fell from the sky. One evening two weeks ago, before she'd invited Hannah over, the Christensen twins from up the street had been sliding around on the icy roads, pretending to skate. Courtney had been halfway down her driveway intending to break every bone in their bodies before she caught herself.

One day, she was going to wake with literal blood on her hands.

The first time it had snowed, she'd driven all the way to her ex-boyfriend's house to murder him. She hadn't remembered the drive. Still couldn't. Fortunately, he lived with people who seemed to understand what was going on.

The place was weird, the people weirder, but they and their magical cats had done their best to help Courtney. They thought they had.

But they'd failed.

Courtney kept intending to call them. Each time, her cell phone would go missing, or die, or the call wouldn't go through. Once she'd gotten her ex, Chase, and he'd laughed at her for trying to call.

Their house was across town. She could drive there today, instead of going home. Maybe they'd take care of her. They'd kept her from harming anyone last time. She might have hurt one of the cats, but it was just a cat, right?

Cats terrified her, but deep down, killing one would rip Courtney apart. She wasn't a killer. Yet this thing in her mind tried to make her into one.

Courtney waited by the side door of the clinic, stealing herself for the cold blast that would come when she opened it. She wore heavy winter boots, solid ones that she had gotten from LL Bean, spending more money than she wanted on snow boots. Living in Lexington, you didn't really need such things. She'd been lucky. Hannah had tried to get some the next week but they'd been sold out. Too many people in Kentucky and Tennessee and Southern Ohio had been purchasing the heavy-duty boots in order to battle the unseasonably cold fall.

It was only November.

One of the other admins hurried over and paused before the door, both she and Courtney preparing as best they could to feel the cold that would eat away at their body heat more quickly than a school of piranha would finish a feast of two adults.

"You guys are lucky," Lori called over to them. Lori was a large woman with short hair who'd been a nurse at the clinic since before Courtney had started. Lori would be expected to continue working. She had a motherly attitude about her that made Courtney want to tell her all about the weird things that were going on with her.

Courtney had tried to talk to Lori once and she'd not been able to spit out a word. Finally, she'd ended up telling Lori that she looked particularly nice that day. A stupid thing. Lori had laughed. Courtney had laughed too and pushed it off on her fatigue. Even that opening hadn't allowed Courtney to say more.

That was one reason she hadn't gotten across town to Chase's. She needed to get there, one way or another.

That last thought warmed her as she thought about how nice it would be to squeeze the life of the people at Chase's, perhaps break some bones, wring the necks of the cats, or maybe kick one across the room. She dreamed of a sharp knife that would allow her to gut the weird guy, Stuart, who seemed somehow in charge even if he didn't live in the house. She wanted to know if his blood still ran red or if it had changed color.

The icy blast of air hit Courtney bringing her back to the present. She followed the admin through the door. She put up her umbrella under the awning wondering why she didn't think that Stuart's blood would be red.

STUART

Stuart felt the falling snow like a drumbeat in his blood. He didn't even have to look out the window with the half-broken, cheap metal shade to see the flakes spinning down from the sky. The hairs on his arm rose, not because of the chill outside—it was warm in the third-floor bedroom he occupied—but because something was happening.

It had snowed since the first big storm in October that had had his seniors at Base Command sending him down to Lexington. The in-between snows had been lighter and hadn't set his blood to thrumming in anticipation or, perhaps, fear.

He'd have been stupid not to be afraid, not after last time. The clowder, that group of people in the house who were all telepathically linked to their very special cats, wanted to believe that they'd taken care of the problem, that the subsequent snows had just been the weather ironing out the weirdness of the sudden drop in temperature and snowstorm in October.

Stuart had known better than to hope. He suspected most of the others did, too, though they didn't want to admit it.

The solid black watcher cat, Trag, curled up on the mattress that lay on the floor. Stuart had picked this particular room, the one the clowder tossed all the stuff they didn't think was needed any longer but couldn't just throw away, because of that mattress. He was used to sleeping on the floor. Tenny had found him some flannel sheets in navy and cream plaid. Anson had an extra comforter, an old purple one with the threads pulling out here and there, probably purchased on sale. It promised more warmth than it offered, but with the flannel sheets, it wasn't bad, along with the extra pink fleece that Drew had come up with.

Stuart had a feeling Drew had picked the blanket up at the store when he'd run out after the first snow stopped. Chances were the color was picked because it was on sale. It was thoughtful of him. Since then Stuart had come to appreciate the extra warmth.

Trag yawned at him and gave him a half-lidded stare. Trag knew what was going on out there. Stuart could almost hear his thoughts, a sort of rumbling train in the back of his mind if he touched the cat. They weren't bond-mates to read each other's minds, though, so communication wasn't reliable. Cats only bonded with one human. Trag should be bonded to Chase, but the creature that had caused the snowfall had influenced Chase in some way.

Chase managed to warn the cat, but since then he'd felt wrong to both Trag and to the healers, Amber and her bond-mate cat, Minnett. Privately, Stuart thought Chase felt more like the slightly alien beings at Base Command than he did like a human. It wasn't something Stuart could talk about. The clowder members knew plenty of things, but they didn't know all the secrets of Base Command, nor were they supposed to, not unless they were found suitable for the job sometime after their bond-mate cat died.

Stuart tried to sink down in meditation. It was a place he often calmed himself, but the snow insisted upon his attention with all the stubbornness of a toddler needing his mommy. It wouldn't let him go.

Things were happening.

He heard footsteps outside the door, probably Julia from the sound, leaving her room to go downstairs. He was becoming used to the normal sounds of the house, the fact that his room didn't have the same level of insulation as his apartment back at Base Command. The scent of coffee permeated the house no matter the time of day. Someone always had a cup freshly made, or so it seemed.

The clowder existed to guard against incursions from other worlds. Just a few blocks away was a portal where those incursions arrived in a park, beneath trees that normally hung heavy with thick green leaves and now huddled barren and stooped against the chill and the periodically falling snow.

Anson was out on watch. Stuart knew Anson had been called in. That was the sort of call he could pick up if he paid attention. Being near Trag helped him focus on those general calls to the cats from Base Command. Temperatures were falling too quickly for this to be a normal storm. They would take no chances on losing another watcher. For all means and purposes, they'd lost Chase since Trag would not re-bond with him.

Watchers watched, as their name suggested, the portals in case something came through. They could push the some-thing back through if need be. If it was too much for them to do so alone, the guardians would assist them. Each watcher worked closely with two guardians who would have his back.

A really large incursion would call out the whole clowder, but for the healer, and, if there was one, the researcher.

Stuart had been a watcher in his day. Those were good days, spent in the Southwest, beneath a sun that usually shone too warmly at midday and beneath a moon that left the small plateau almost frosty. The moment the sun started setting, leaving the day in deep reds and blues, the heat dissipated from the rocks making it the best part of the day. Too early for the snakes and insects but too late for the hottest moments.

If this creature, probably one of the frost witches of legend, had its way, that portal, too, would be buried beneath ice and snow soon enough. Stuart had no idea how long it would take to get that far. Ultimately, it appeared that no one had found a way of stopping the frost witches. Each world had been destroyed, the life force of the world eaten away so that nothing was left but the cold void of space.

Stuart wondered if the eating away took weeks or months or years. However long it took, it was probably the length of time he could measure his lifespan. Trag paused in his washing to regard him. The cat had found a nice nest next to the pillow Amber had donated, his black fur in stark contrast to the pink and purple of the blankets.

Sighing, Stuart stood up. He was going to be needed. He knew he wasn't ready for this, but who of them was? Base Command was running scared, his direct boss, Darla more irritable each time she called, which was saying something.

Stuart might intellectually know how bad things were, but Darla's increasing irritation brought it home and sent shivers of fear down his spine every time his phone rang.

COURTNEY

The snow on the streets was packed and solid. On the main roads, the pavement remained bare though the snow was attempting to get a foothold there, too. It would overnight, of that Courtney had no doubt.

She drove her little silver Scion XA carefully. She'd gotten as far as Richmond Road on New Circle Road before she realized she was heading to Chase's house rather than her own home. She decided to just continue straight ahead to head home—after all, there was a reason the highway was called "New Circle Road."

While others might be white-knuckling the drive, and Courtney's hands were certainly hugging the steering wheel tighter than usual, she didn't feel particularly afraid. The thing inside her, the thing that wasn't her that wanted to go to Chase's house and kill all his housemates and their cats, needed her. It wouldn't let her die.

Heat rushed from the air vents just barely keeping up with the temperature outside. The windows had fog around the edges but her defroster allowed her to see out, though it was a near thing. If she had a fancy car like the Range Rover

Weird Stuart had, she'd be sitting pretty. Probably the radio would play songs that didn't sound so filled with static like hers had been for the last two weeks.

Courtney let the anger fill her. It was warm, comforting somehow. As she slowed the car when the road angled down, becoming a main throughway with traffic lights at the cross streets rather than off-ramps and overpasses, the anger began to dissipate, leaving her cold and her arms heavy with fatigue.

Her eyelids started feeling as if she needed sleep and Courtney looked for a place to pull in and rest, just for a minute. Her sister didn't live far from there.

She could go to Payton's house and settle in there, though first, she'd have to kill Payton. Her sister was so proud of her knife set so there was sure to be something plenty sharp to cut out her heart and intestines.

Courtney gulped back bile, tears forming at the edges of her eyes. She didn't know how she could even think such thoughts, particularly not about her sister. She adored Payton.

No longer trusting herself to find a place to pull over, Courtney kept driving. Better to fall asleep at the wheel and die than kill her sister. If that's what it took to keep her family safe, then she'd do it.

The sudden rush of self-hatred helped the fatigue. Courtney made a mental note that when she had any sort of emotional rush, anger, or disgust, she was warmer, stronger, readier to take on whatever it was. When she felt normal, not particularly angry or sad but just ordinary, her body got colder and sometimes weaker.

"Courtney…" a static-filled voice said from the radio. Courtney flipped the button off. She didn't want to hear it. She didn't want to hear it describe how to kill Payton or Chase or anyone else. She wanted to get home and go to sleep. Maybe she could tie herself up or something. She quickly tossed that idea. If she could tie herself up, she could untie herself when she was under the creature's influence. Besides, she had no rope.

She turned off New Circle and threaded her way around the northern part of Lexington. The snow was falling harder. More people were driving themselves home. Schools had probably closed early so some would be picking up their kids.

The McDonald's on the corner was doing a good business with so many cars in the drive-thru that Courtney couldn't have turned into the parking lot if she had wanted to. The bright colors of the building and the interior orange-cast lights drew her. People waited in lines inside. She would love to be part of that crowd, safe with others around her, where someone would stop her if she tried murdering someone with a plastic knife.

The light turned green and Courtney continued on to her home. She used side streets, the pavement covered with snow, some packed with a few tracks, others not so much. When her back tires slipped a bit, she held on and hoped, though she wasn't sure if she were hoping for an accident to leave her to freeze or an accident to kill her immediately. Either way, during her drive, she became more certain that she had to die.

When her home appeared before her and she drove into the garage, Courtney closed the garage door, intending to sit in her car until the exhaust fumes overcame her. It might even be considered an accident and her family wouldn't need to know of her desperation.

After about thirty seconds, before her body had any time to register that it wasn't getting the oxygen it needed, perhaps long before the exhaust had eaten up the oxygen, the engine sputtered and died.

Courtney put her head down on the steering wheel and closed her eyes against the tears that wanted to form. She couldn't even kill herself with this thing inside her.

Drawing in a breath, she grabbed her purse and walked into the house. She'd have a snack and try and decide what to do next. Just because she couldn't kill herself the first time she tried, didn't mean she couldn't succeed later.

Her cell phone rang as she put her purse down on the kitchen table. She looked at it, hoping for Payton or Hannah or someone she could talk to about the snow and maybe forget the nightmare her life had become. Instead, the caller-ID showed Amber Ryan, from Chase's clowder house.

Courtney wanted to answer but her fingers stubbornly refused to allow her to do so. She merely put the phone aside and started making herself a plate of nachos. She'd eat them in front of the TV while she re-binged Vampire Diaries. After all, at least those monsters were good, sort of. Even Klaus, in his weird way. And even if they weren't good, she at least understood them which was more than she could say about the thing that existed inside her.

*A*mber made notes on her computer down in her basement office. Minnett, her bond-mate cat, lay in a bed beneath the desk, her body heat warming Amber's feet, which felt chilled even through her heavy socks and slippers. The slab basement floor was always cold, despite the thickly layered carpet that covered much of that level.

The overhead light was bright, one bulb beginning to flicker, probably in its last stages of life. She'd need to change that soon, or perhaps Drew would do it for her. He was good at things like that.

Laughter came from the other room as her clowder mates, Drew, Matt, and Chase played pool while keeping an eye on the backyard and the falling snow. Amber didn't trust Chase and knew that the others didn't trust him either. Not since the last snowfall when something had happened to him.

She'd looked into how often a bond-mate cat had had to severe a bond and it wasn't something that was taken lightly. In most cases, it was done temporarily and as soon as the threat had passed or the human had been treated, the cat initiated the bond once more. She found nothing about the bond-mate cats not re-initiating the bond due to lack of trust. Their own Trag would go down in the annals of Base Command and perhaps even those of Cat Home.

Amber looked over her notes on Chase from before the snowfall in October. She used both Eastern and Western diagnostic terms. Chase's body hadn't changed in any concrete way via either paradigm. Even when she looked him over, she didn't see anything that had changed, only had the feeling that there was something she was missing. Minnett mentioned a fleeting shadow, but it was like the shadows you see out of the corner of your eye that disappear the moment you try and focus on them.

Nothing Amber did or tested made any difference.

They hadn't gotten rid of the frost witch or witches. Were there two, one for Courtney and one for Chase, or were both Courtney and Chase infected by one frost witch? Amber didn't know. Courtney wouldn't return her calls, even to check-in. She didn't even text which was more than a little irritating.

Anxiety rose each time Courtney didn't respond. Amber wondered if Courtney couldn't respond. She'd gone so far as to check obituaries online. Courtney had a Facebook presence and posted regularly. Her profile wasn't very locked down and Amber followed Courtney to make sure she was okay or as okay as Amber could ascertain via social media. She felt like a cyber-stalker, and, to be honest, she probably was, but if Courtney wouldn't respond or perhaps couldn't respond to Amber's outreach, maybe she'd say something or give something away on Facebook.

Perhaps Amber had failed Courtney in the same way she failed Chase. At least Chase was at the clowder house where they could monitor him. He got antsy to go outside every time the snow started to fall. Last time, Fin had had to physically restrain him.

Back in October as soon as the first big snow had stopped falling, Julia had gone out and repaired the hurricane shutters they had on Chase's bedroom window and re-closed them. She put on the heaviest-duty lock she could find to try and prevent people outside from trying to break into his room.

The other shutters were open. Amber suspected that Julia and Cari had gone out to the covered front porch and closed the shutters across the big windows on the front room. Those were the easiest to get to and made the house look far less welcoming. If people were out wandering in the snow and guided to the clowder house to make trouble, even having one window covered was a good thing.

Drew had purchased a bunch of plywood that sat in the garage in case they couldn't get out to cover the other windows. They'd been lucky to be able to last time. Fortunately, they'd had an inkling that their house would be targeted. Unfortunately, the weather forecasters never seemed to know when snow would fall.

Anson and Matt took turns watching the portal. They dressed in heavy layers and carried umbrellas and even had a small tent which they set up in the park to keep the snow off of them and their bond-mate cats.

Normally, the watchers would detect at least one incursion a week. In a slow month, a week might be skipped. Nothing had come through since the frost witches unless you counted one dead fire dingo that came through about the same time everything had started. Amber felt as if the other worlds knew that there was something wrong in this world and were avoiding it lest they attract the notice of the witches themselves.

Amber sighed, putting her hands over her face. She hated

feeling helpless. She hated feeling as if the solution to the problem rested with her. She was the healer. When something happened to one of the clowder, she was the one who had to fix it, along with Minnett. Normally, Minnett had ideas, but in this case, she, too, was stumped. They'd tried everything.

Minnett had been in contact with the command cats at Base Command but they'd offered no new insights, either. Why did it have to happen to her clowder? Why not one somewhere else, where she could study and research, and Minnett could offer suggestions telepathically but someone else would have to put those things in practice?

Why would anyone start a world takeover in Lexington, Kentucky?

"Because that was the portal that opened from their world," Minnett told her telepathically.

"How does that even work?" Amber asked. She didn't understand the world portals.

"I believe Drew imagines the worlds as bubbles floating around in space and sometimes they bump up against each other. It's a good analogy," Minnett said. *"However, you must also think of the bubbles as turning the way the earth turns so that other bubbles on collision courses will hit different areas. These aren't planets in the typical universal space you are thinking of, but worlds in other universes that inhabit all the layers of reality. Even there, they have certain vectors and speeds. It's why the portals are not static. Where you end up when you pass through one changes as the movements of the worlds change."*

"But watcher cats can send back creatures to their world. Stuart made sure to find a dead space to send the jars I filled with the glop we pulled out of Courtney and Chase," Amber said.

"We can set the portals to where we want," Minnett said patiently, the pause aching for Amber's next question.

"And how do you know where something is if it's always chang-

ing?" Amber asked. She wasn't sure she cared. What she wanted to know was why them? Had there been a plan to invade this world or was it just accidentally found?

"*We just know,*" Minnett said. "*I can feel the worlds and their placements. It's like your sense of direction. Some humans have a stronger sense of it than others. Watcher cats have the strongest sense of where the worlds are. Humans, like Stuart, know how to work the math.*"

"*Is there any way to figure out where the frost witch might have come from?*" Amber asked.

"*If we knew when it appeared, we could guess. Unfortunately, we think it remained hidden for about a week. It appears to Trag that something happened during a specific watch shift that Chase had a week before the first snow. However, Trag doesn't have any memory of what happened during the time he feels his memories are blocked so we can't be certain of what was close. Trust me when I say that Base Command and Cat Home are doing their best to coordinate and perhaps assist Cat Home's protected networked worlds from becoming prey to the frost witches ever again.*"

"In other words, they'll leave us and protect what they can," Amber thought. Cynical but she didn't expect much more.

"*We're linked by the portals. If the witches succeed here, chances are they will hop from one world to the next and finally to Cat Home itself. They will not be leaving this world to fend for itself,*" Minnett said.

Which meant that not only was saving this world, her world, on her shoulders but so was saving all the worlds. Not exactly what Amber needed in her life.

"*No one expects you to do this single-handed,*" Minnett said. "*You have the entire backing of Base Command and Cat Home doing research for you. It's quite unprecedented.*"

Amber felt a sort of pride from Minnett that they were the focus of something so important. If only she had

Minnett's capacity for complete and utter self-confidence that she wouldn't screw up and destroy the known worlds.

Before, when she'd bonded with Minnett, Amber had loved the powers it gave her and the extra healing abilities. It made her a pretty kick-ass acupuncturist. Now, though… Now her knowledge and powers didn't seem nearly enough to do what was needed and the responsibility weighed heavy on her shoulders.

DREW

*D*rew listened to the bump and clack of the billiards after Chase broke for the next game. Chase and Matt were good players, but Fin was really the player to beat. He wasn't down there that afternoon. Instead, he was upstairs resting in case something happened during the night.

Matt had beaten Drew in the last game and was now playing Chase. Drew would rotate in and play the winner of the next game. Drew was a decent enough player but he didn't have the practice the other two men had. Now that someone always needed to keep an eye on Chase, he'd been playing more pool and his game had really improved.

Chase had on some country music station and someone crooned about love gone wrong in the background. Drew let the sounds flow over him, trying not to pick up on the emotion in the song. Lately, he'd felt more emotionally vulnerable, as if in offering his energy to Amber he had opened himself to feeling more.

"You probably did," Mack commented in the background. Drew's big orange bond-mate cat was upstairs snoozing on

the sofa. He said he was watching the backyard, but Drew knew the cat had both eyes closed.

"*I'm psychic,*" Mack said, annoyed.

Drew couldn't argue. The cats were telepathic and each of them had different powers, most of them dealing with what humans would call psychic phenomena. Therefore, Mack was telling the truth and not completely pulling his leg.

Drew leaned against one of the club chairs that were placed strategically around the room along with small round tables that restaurants would call two-tops. One table held two beers, Chase's can a cheap Budweiser, Matt's a Fat Tire. Drew held his own bottle of Guinness and took a sip, holding the liquid, savoring the flavor of hops in his mouth for a second as he watched the snowfall.

The deep gray clouds outside poured flakes from their bellies, dousing the city. Directly outside the main room was a patio covered by the balcony above. Some snow sneaked through the wood slats and covered the concrete in rather neat and tidy rows. The grass beyond was fully covered in white and the trees near the edge of the lawn half bent over, the tips of their branches already touching the ground.

No wind stirred any of the bushes or blew the snow off the bony branches to ease the weight of the tree's burden.

Drew sighed. He heard someone hurrying down the stairs, probably from the second floor. The fast, almost robotic tread sounded like Stuart. The front door opened up there. Drew thought he felt the chill all the way in the basement, but it had to be his imagination.

As Drew turned, Chase looked over at him and grinned as he rubbed some chalk on the tip of his cue. Behind him, a picture of cats playing poker stared at Drew, each cat with the same sort of cunning smile that Chase gave him.

"Better go up," Chase said.

"Why?" Drew asked.

He heard voices, wondered who would be trying to go out. Stuart more than most would understand the danger.

"Courtney is here," Mack said.

Matt paused in lining up his shot. At some point, Chase must have missed a shot and it was Matt's turn. Drew hadn't been paying attention, busy watching the snowfall as if it needed his supervision.

Chase gave Drew a bigger grin. "Told ya." It was as if Chase heard Mack, which wasn't possible. The telepathic link was exclusive to one person. Even Stuart didn't really hear the bond-mate cats, though he said he heard white noise and could sometimes pick upon human thoughts.

The idea that Chase had more power than any of the rest of them chilled Drew. It should chill all of them.

Drew set his Guinness down on the empty coaster on the far table and walked up the stairs to see what was going on. Climbing the carpet-covered stairs, he was aware that it was colder up there. The door had to still be open.

When he reached the top of the stairs, he walked into the great room, which held the kitchen, a large eating area, and a seating area that faced a large fireplace that currently had a fire going. This one was gas. In an emergency, they had wood for the real fireplace in the front room.

Cari was at the breakfast nook, leaning forward, craning her neck to see the front entry.

Drew turned the corner. Kayley stood to the side, probably watching the front room, though Drew didn't understand why. The hurricane shutters were closed across the windows making it impossible to see out. She held her tablet, as always. Stuart stood at the door and was looking out.

"I heard Courtney was here," Drew said. He didn't see her.

"She's still in her car," Kayley said.

Drew nodded. He went to the door, folding his arms across his body to try and stay warm, though that ship had probably sailed. Looking out the door, standing next to Stuart who always smelled of something alien to Drew's nose, he had a hard time making out the silver Scion in the falling snow. It blended in with the shadows and clouds around the house.

Courtney got out of the car about that time. She had been opening an umbrella to keep the snow off of her as much as possible. Last time she'd appeared half-dressed, barefoot, and in pajamas and a tank top, marching across the snow as if it were no big deal. This time she had her umbrella, a small duffle bag, and a purse. She was dressed in a ski jacket with a knit cap on her head under the hood. Her feet were shod in heavy-duty beige and brown snow boots.

She hurried to the porch, clearly worried about the snow.

"I need help," she said, standing there, looking at the two men. Drew stepped back to let her in.

Stuart hesitated a moment but then moved back a bit so that she could pass. "How can we help?" he asked.

Courtney spent a moment closing her umbrella and then setting it in the corner. "I keep hearing voices. Telling me to kill people. This afternoon, I took a baseball bat to my neighbor's car because I wanted him to come out so I could beat them. To death. He was yelling at me from his porch and had a phone. I realized what was happening and went in the house and grabbed a few things and came here. You need to tie me up again."

Stuart raised an eyebrow.

Drew said nothing waiting.

"Well?" Courtney asked. "You have a kitchen around the corner. I can feel the knives. Like they're calling me. I want..." she trailed off and shook her head. Drew could imagine what she wanted.

"I can't take you downstairs. It's too close to Chase," Stuart said. "I believe there's room on the third floor?"

"She can use the same room she used last time," Cari called from the kitchen. Cari and Julia used that room to store extra stuff. The two of them shared a large oblong room over the front of the house with two dormer windows. A small room sat in the corner of the upper floor next to it. It was one of the smallest bedrooms in the house, hence the use for storage.

They had put Courtney up there for a few nights after the last snow because it was also the room furthest away from Chase's room down in the opposite corner of the basement.

"Is there a lock?" Courtney asked. "From the outside?"

"We'll work something out," Stuart said. "Let's go up and we'll have Amber come examine you."

Stuart gave Kayley a look and told her to be sure the cats let Amber know what was happening. Drew's Mack could have done the same but no one ever thought he was useful. Drew sighed. He held out a hand to take Courtney's bag for her.

COURTNEY

The baseball bat was the last straw. Courtney had finished the plate of nachos and sipped a Dr. Pepper—there was no beer in the fridge—and was sitting on the sofa, her feet curled under her. She'd been pleasantly tired, letting her eyes start to drift closed. It wasn't as if she hadn't seen every single episode of the Vampire Diaries at least four times. Some people watched Desperate Housewives. Courtney watched Vampire Diaries.

She had felt cradled in the soft, comfortable sofa, the afghan that smelled of Payton's baby powder scent, the lingering smells of nacho cheese and salty chips, the low voices of the television surrounding her. The images behind her eyelids turned to red flowers flashing closer and closer to her. Courtney's half-conscious mind found the flowers fascinating and she tried to get closer to them.

She dreamed she was in a field of blood-red flowers, their heads falling to the side. The field was silent and still as a grave. Courtney turned around, wondering what the place was. Deep down, it felt wrong. She had no desire to run. She

25

wanted to open her eyes and find herself back on her sofa but she couldn't make her eyelids work.

Still, she struggled against the deep sleep that had overcome her, more like a drugged unconsciousness than a true sleep, until finally, she'd pulled her eyelids open. She stood in front of the Lewis's big black Dodge Ram truck with the crew cab. She held an old gray and black baseball bat which she kept in her bedroom, a remnant of her days in girls' softball and now a means of protection should someone break-in.

Courtney didn't know how she had come to grab it. Her feet were cold and damp in only her slippers. Snow fell around her. The car alarm bellowed at her, letting her know that the damage to the black paint on the side and the smashed window had likely come from her bat.

Jason Lewis was on the porch, yelling something at her. Courtney couldn't quite make out the words over the sound of the alarm. She hung her head and ran back to her house, still holding the bat.

Her front door hung open. The television still played. Courtney ran inside, dropping the bat on the floor. She slammed the door shut, turned the lock, and leaned back against the door. What had she been doing? There was a moment when she wanted to run over to Jason and slam the bat into him.

She'd longed for the feel of flesh bending beneath the weight of the bat, listening for the crunch of his bones, watching blood flow from his head. Courtney shook her head to get rid of the images.

The bat lay on the floor, calling to her hands. Courtney kicked it away, water splattering from her soaked slippers.

Her hair dripped on her shoulders. She'd been out in the snow and in the warmth of the house, it was melting. Sudden cold gripped her body and Courtney moved from the door.

The movement propelled her across the room. She reached the remote and quickly turned off the television. She ran to her bedroom to change socks and put on her winter boots.

She changed out of her light sweater and put on a heavy sweatshirt. Her jeans were damp but not horribly so. She didn't want to take the time to change them.

She grabbed a small duffle bag she'd gotten as a shopping gift and tossed in her phone charger. Pulling open drawers, she tossed in underwear and some socks. A couple of shirts and a pair of sweats. In the bathroom, Courtney pulled out a little bathroom travel kit.

Carrying the blue duffle, she hurried to the kitchen where she found her purse and her phone. She went to the office to grab her tablet and stuffed it inside the duffle. Putting on her heavy coat, Courtney didn't even double-check the lights in the house, though normally she was obsessive about doing so. She needed to get to Chase's.

The idea of Chase's house was hers. She longed to be among people who could keep her from hurting other people, maybe put her in restraints as they had last time. It was the only way she could trust herself.

While Courtney feared she might accidentally drive her car to her parents' or her sister's or some random store where she'd attempt to murder complete strangers, the creature inside her seemed pleased at Courtney's decision to go to Chase's.

It wanted to murder all of the humans and cats. The longing to destroy the cats, to wipe them from the face of the earth bubbled up in her. Courtney pushed it down.

As she drove, perhaps a bit too fast for the weather, passing Jason Lewis who still stood on his front porch, a cell phone in hand, Courtney worried she was being led into a trap. The idea of killing Chase, his housemates, and the cats warmed her in a way that the thoughts of killing Jason Lewis didn't.

It would be fun to kill her neighbor and he would die soon enough but it was important that she kill Chase's housemates.

Courtney considered turning around and heading back home. Except she'd tried that earlier and she'd done damage to her neighbor's truck. It wasn't bad enough for the police to arrest her, though if she walked out talking about hearing voices telling her to smash up his truck and perhaps his face, they might put her on a 72 hour psychiatric hold.

It would only be 72 hours and then she'd be right back where she was now, perhaps worse off. The thing inside her was getting stronger. Better to warn Chase's group now, before it got so strong that they wouldn't be able to stop her. Courtney didn't think she could stop herself.

The snow had been coming down harder, but as she got closer to the house and had to navigate a few hills and curves to wend her way to that part of town, the flakes lightened a bit, probably to help keep her safe. The thing inside her controlled the snow.

Courtney had known that deep down, but on her drive over, she became sure of it. When she pulled into the driveway of the clowder house, she noted the silver shutters across the front window. The other windows appeared unprotected.

As she sat there thinking, someone opened the front door. Weird Stuart stepped out onto the front porch and looked at her. The snow fell harder, like it was angry at his appearance.

Courtney dug around in the front seat of her little Scion, momentarily unable to find her umbrella. Then it was there, in her hands. She found the knit cap she kept in the car, not her favorite headwear, but she kept it there in case she forgot to wear a nicer one. She pulled that on and put up the hood of her ski jacket.

She was ready to face the house. She grabbed her duffle and her purse.

"*Kill them all,*" the voice whispered in her mind.

Courtney tried to keep a small smile on her face, one that she hoped didn't look too much like a grimace. She had no desire to scare them.

Stuart had stepped back into the house by the time she got to the steps. No footprints marred the white perfection, though she knew hers had done so behind her. It made her sad for just an instant.

The heat of the house rushed out to greet her. Once inside the door, Courtney noted that Weird Stuart, the big guy, Drew, and the young woman named Kayley were all there waiting on her. The house smelled, as always, of coffee and meals long since eaten and beneath that an acidic scent Courtney associated with cats. Except for the latter, the house was welcoming. Not a single cat came to greet her. In fact, Courtney suspected they had all run to rooms further into the house, lest she be there to murder them.

The cats were indeed smarter than average.

Instead of punching Stuart and hitting him with her duffle, Courtney took a deep breath, attempting to get words out, words that wouldn't come. Finally, "I need help."

Whatever Stuart expected from Courtney it hadn't been for her to ask for their help. She'd been avoiding Amber's calls for weeks. She hadn't responded to texts. He'd even driven by her house and rung the bell. Though the blinds had moved slightly while he stood at the door, no one had come out. A neighbor across the way had wandered out to get her mail so instead of walking around the house, Stuart had gone back to his car.

Neighbors could be protective, at least the neighbors Stuart remembered from so very long ago. Even now, when he watched the news, he heard about things like neighborhood watches and more formal ways of looking out for people living nearby. In his day that was just being part of a community.

Yet, here Courtney was, asking for help. Cari was already suggesting a room as if Courtney remaining with them was a foregone conclusion. Stuart understood the necessity, but his intuition didn't like Courtney and Chase being under the same roof, not with the snow falling the way it was. Bad enough if she had come last week, but today…

Of course, the snow was probably bothering her.

Stuart climbed the wood stairs, a hand lightly on the rail. He didn't pause on the second floor, barely acknowledging the light that escaped from the library and into the hallway. The cats waited in there, using their senses to attempt to determine what it was that Courtney wanted. Even Trag had joined them and of all the cats, Stuart could feel him the most strongly, as if they were half-way to bonding together already, though neither of them had asked for the relationship.

The stairs to the third floor were covered in the same beige carpet that covered the upper floors and the basement. Only the first floor and the stairs leading up to the second had hardwood. The hallway on the third floor was narrower, the ceiling angled just slightly, letting anyone walking up there know that this was supposed to be an attic.

Stuart's room was across the way. Julia and Cari shared the room above the library. The one Cari had suggested for Courtney was down at the end. Courtney stayed right behind him, so close he could feel the warmth of her breath on his back. It made the hairs on the back of his neck stand up, and when they were nearly to the door and Courtney went to pass him, brushing his arm, Stuart was tempted to put her in a stranglehold. The fact that he didn't took every ounce of the discipline his former bond-mate Stardust had insisted he acquire.

"In here," Stuart said, moving out of the way, hoping the movement of his arm could be taken as a gesture to enter. From the look on Courtney's face, he suspected he'd failed. Even Drew was glowering at him, although Drew always glowered at him as if the incursion of the frost witches was all Stuart's fault.

Courtney slipped inside. She'd spent a couple of nights in the room last time she'd stayed at the clowder house.

"Are you sure there's no lock?" she asked.

Julia came out of her room, yawning. She was fully dressed, though, and her short dark hair was combed tidily. Her breath smelled of peppermint. Stuart suspected she'd just been roused by her bond-mate Axel.

"I'll be out here," Julia said. "I'll make sure you don't leave. Axel will warn the others if something happens to me, okay?"

Stuart doubted that Courtney could physically take Julia but the fact that she was influenced or infected by the frost witch meant she might be able to subdue any of the clowder. The fact that she was there at all put them all in danger. Of course, if she weren't there, they would still be in danger, but so would other people.

"I'll have Amber come up to examine you," Stuart said. "Why don't you go in and get comfortable. We'll be back in a few."

Drew glared at him as Courtney closed the door. All the doors were painted a creamy white. All the doors along the hall were closed but the light color kept the hallway somewhat bright, though they needed to turn on a light.

"Do you think Amber's up to it?" Drew asked. He stood too close to Stuart.

Julia made herself comfortable on the floor, pulling out her phone from a pocket in the gray yoga pants she wore.

"Does it matter?" Stuart asked. He didn't bother to look at Drew. He continued walking quickly down the hallway. He wanted to speak to Amber on the first floor, far enough away from Chase that he wouldn't hear and far enough away from Courtney that she wouldn't hear them either.

"What do you mean, does it matter?" Drew practically spit. "How can it not?"

"Someone has to examine her to see what's going on. Amber is the only person in the clowder who can," Stuart said.

"You do examinations all the time." Drew wasn't going to let up. Stuart had found his protectiveness tiresome but normal when he'd first arrived. After several weeks of this, he was beginning to find him irritating.

"I can't see what Amber and Minnett see," Stuart said. "My examinations are different. Which, I'm sure you recall, we've talked about this before."

Drew said nothing as they started down the stair to the first floor. Amber was in the front room on the large sofa, holding her phone and typing on it.

"Courtney's here?" she asked. Or maybe it was a statement. Minnett would have told her Courtney was there. If not the cat, then surely Kayley who was back in one of the armchairs near the window. She appeared to be listening to something outside rather than watching. Of course, there was no window to watch out of there, unless she stood on a stool and looked out the front door.

"She is," Stuart settled on the sofa. "We need to go examine her."

"What if I don't find anything, like with Chase?" Amber said. "We know there's something, but I can't see it. It's not like that with Matt. He feels normal."

"Maybe we need to go on gut feelings and see what Courtney feels like, particularly compared to how Chase feels. It might give us ideas on how the infections, if that's what we're calling them, differ between them."

"I think it's more like possession," Amber said. "The people who came to the house were probably influenced. They seemed mostly normal after the snow stopped. I've talked to the Martins next door, twice. They had a couple of days of being really tired but seem better now. And they don't remember being at our place during the snow."

"Then possession. Of course, as we're talking about two people, that means we have more than one frost witch,"

Stuart pointed out. He liked the idea of an infection, a small thing that could be killed. Possession made the witch more of a creature, a highly sentient creature who acted for a specific reason and not just a viral thing that might force people to its will but had no real motivation other than to procreate.

Desires came in all forms with sentience. Did the frost witches just desire the destruction of a world or did they desire something from that destruction that would make them act in a certain way? Given the way people had been influenced, he had a feeling he wasn't going to like knowing what it was they desired.

Amber didn't feel up to examining Courtney, but Stuart made it clear in his talk that she needed to. He'd be there. Walking up the stairs, Amber worried about Minnett. Courtney had hurt the cat, and if not for Drew's quick thinking, she might have been injured worse. Drew was a nice enough guy but he wasn't a healer. She didn't trust that he'd know that something was wrong unless Minnett was in dire states.

"He'd hear about it from Mack," Minnett assured her. *"You're too hard on him."*

If Drew was going to be in her medic room, helping her as he liked to do, then he needed to be on top of his game, all the time. The medic room was life and death. Courtney's examination required they all be at their best and that Amber could trust everyone. It was bad enough that she had to work with Stuart. She trusted him not at all. Drew followed them up and would no doubt insert himself into the room on the pretext of taking care of her.

"You are too hard on him," Minnett repeated. *"He was chosen."* As if being chosen should make Amber think more

highly of him. Drew had been a good guardian and Amber was sorry that he and Mack were forced into retirement when Mack hit ten, but that didn't mean Drew was good in the medic room. He might be courageous, plunging in where things scared him, but that didn't mean he covered his nervousness well.

Minnett grumbled in the back of her mind. Amber wasn't going to argue. She needed to focus on Courtney. Julia sat on the floor outside the room. Courtney's door was closed.

"Nothing's gone on," Julia said without being asked. She didn't even look up from her phone. Amber wanted to ask how she'd know. She bit back the comment, knowing she was feeling bitchy simply because of the stress.

Amber knocked, not sure if that was appropriate or not. Better to start polite. Maybe Courtney's human-side would remain in control if she felt less threatened. If niceness didn't work, Amber, Stuart, and the bond-mate cats could always find another way to deal with her. Whatever that could be.

While Amber had to admit it would be easier to just toss Courtney through the portal, stressed though she might be, she didn't feel good about killing someone. And Courtney would have to die. That would leave them with Chase. Even if she could sentence Courtney to death, could she sentence someone who had once been a friend? Amber couldn't in good conscience call him a friend any longer. He no longer acted that way.

"Come in!" Courtney called.

Amber opened the door. The day bed was across the room from the door, pressed up against the wall, under a window. Soft cream and teal covers covered the bed and five throw pillows in cream, teal, or a striped combination lined the back. Courtney curled up near the foot of the bed against the white wooden arm, a teal pillow behind her back. Other than that, the bed was perfectly made.

A white wicker chair sat off in the far corner of the room next to an antique white dresser. Courtney's blue duffle rested on the chair, partly opened. Her purse lay on the dresser. A small bathroom sat around the corner out of Amber's line of sight, along with a decent-sized closet that was filled with odds and ends Julia and Cari didn't have room for in the bigger room next door.

Courtney looked up at Amber and Stuart expectantly. "What do you need me to do?" she finally asked.

Amber looked at Stuart. Minnett hung back in the doorway, safely behind Amber, as if worried about what might happen when she crossed the threshold. Through the blinds that had been raised, Amber watched the snow falling, remembering a time when she'd actually liked watching snowfall.

"Maybe lay down?" Amber said. She hated the question mark at the end of her sentence. She should be more certain of herself. Instead, she was tentative.

Courtney scooted around and lay down on her back, head on the main pillow, her feet, now where she'd been sitting. Amber noticed the heavy blue socks on her feet. The boots weren't there, perhaps left at the entry or maybe put away in the closet.

Stuart flowed down into a cross-legged position, a hand resting on Courtney's foot. Amber knelt down and got comfortable, far less elegantly than Stuart. Minnett came up and sat between them. Stuart took Amber's hand as she placed her own hand on Courtney's abdomen, raising Courtney's sweatshirt just a bit.

Courtney giggled a little, probably because Amber's hand was chilly enough to feel cold against the warmth of her belly. In fact, the warmth suggested a light fever though Courtney showed no other outward signs of illness.

Amber frowned as she closed her eyes, preparing to

examine Courtney on the energetic spectrum. She had an idea before sinking into the spectrum.

"Wait," Amber thought at Minnett. She pulled her hand away from Stuart. He raised an eyebrow.

Amber held Courtney's hand and placed three fingers of her opposite hand on Courtney's left wrist, taking pulses in the fashion she had learned in acupuncture school. Each of her fingers told her something about a different energetic aspect of Courtney's body. When Amber switched to the other wrist, she'd learn about different things on the other side of the body.

She pressed her fingers more deeply in different areas, testing the way in which the pulses responded and what she felt. All of Courtney's pulses felt so strong Amber wondered if she was feeling superficial pulses. The right side closest to the wrist was the most common place to feel that sort of pulse. Feeling it in all positions on the left was unusual.

Standing, so she could reach Courtney's other wrist without bringing the arm across Courtney's body—something to avoid when taking pulses—Amber felt those pulses. They weren't as strong, nor did they feel superficial. If anything, they were weak. A normal weakness of someone who had worked too hard and eaten poorly. Maybe a bit worse than normal for someone of Courtney's age.

Amber let go and settled back. She took Stuart's hand without saying anything and closed her eyes. She felt Minnett's mind with hers, sinking into the energetic field of Courtney's body.

Normally, she saw the organs, sometimes in color, sometimes just as a sort of outline. It was a little different each time. Courtney's energetic body appeared filled with black and gray clouds. Amber could see nothing. She wondered if Stuart was seeing more clearly.

"*What about you?*" Amber thought at Minnett.

"Just dark clouds, like you," Minnett said.

Floating through the black and gray clouds felt slimy as if she were swimming in sewer water. Amber prepared to sink deeper, though she resisted, feeling as if her head might submerge into the dank waters of the sewer, the repulsive waste circling and pressing itself against her lips and perhaps even flowing up her nose.

Once in the energetic realm, where she would normally note further, deeper levels of infection or disease, Amber saw only more blackness. Not even clouds. Just nothing.

A pale light flashed in the distance. Something in the light terrified her, sending her fleeing through Courtney's energetic body as fast as possible. Unfortunately, like swimming in sewage sludge, it took longer than it should have.

A stab of ice pierced Amber's body, in her chest and torso, causing her heart to hurt, like heartburn or a heart attack. Momentarily stunned, Amber froze in her retreat, uncertain what to do.

Another stab of ice pierced her through her head, feeling like the worst headache she'd ever had. If she hadn't already paused in her energetic flight, she'd have done so then. The pain ate through her head, the central ache forcing its way outward towards her ears and eyes. This was the sort of pain that would make someone wish for death, or at least make *her* wish for death.

The pain disoriented her. Amber couldn't remember where she was fleeing or how to get out of Courtney's energetic field.

Then, she felt someone pulling at her from a distance. Finally, she felt nothing at all, though she thought she heard Minnett calling her name but from a very long way away.

DREW

$\mathcal{D}$rew hurried forward as Amber slumped backward. Minnett leaped away from Courtney, tail fluffed as if she were ready to do battle. Stuart was already moving to help Amber, but from his angle, even as fast as he was, Amber would hit the floor before he got there.

Drew caught her, easing her down so that she rested on the floor. Courtney had her eyes closed and appeared to be resting easily.

"What happened?" Drew asked.

Stuart didn't answer. He was focused on Courtney, touching her hand, then her head. Courtney didn't respond.

Drew pulled Amber away from the daybed, straightening her legs so that she wouldn't be so uncomfortable. Her body was heavy and her limbs as loose as a poorly sewn ragdoll.

"Minnett says that she and Amber were exiting Courtney's energetic field when Amber cried out. Minnett exited, expecting Amber to have followed, but she hadn't. Stuart apparently pulled Amber out with him as he exited. Minnett experienced nothing except to say that Courtney's energy is black and foggy," Mack said.

Glaring at Stuart and Courtney, Drew pulled Amber further away from the bed. Stuart should have known better than to force Amber to try and heal this woman. Except she wasn't even trying to heal her. This was just an examination or was supposed to be.

"An examination," Mack said, *"that's all. Stuart's the reason Amber is even back in her body. You might not like him but he does not wish us ill."*

"He'll destroy the clowder house if he destroys the portal," Drew said. *"He's willing to do that."*

"He is Base Command," Mack replied easily as if that would explain everything.

Drew didn't care. He needed to fight something real, not this shadow and snow shit. How did you fight snow? If being angry at Stuart and the possibility that he'd destroy the clowder helped him fight, he'd stay angry.

"Let me," Stuart said, moving Drew's hands off of Amber's body.

"What?" Drew snapped.

"I need to examine her," Stuart said.

"You should have examined Courtney first," he said, though he dropped his hands, letting Stuart deal with Amber.

"I don't have the ability to go to the depths that Amber did. If I had felt Courtney was a danger to her, I would not have let her do the examination. Next time, we'll know that even when Courtney consciously cooperates, she isn't fully in control," Stuart said calmly, almost as if he didn't care how Drew felt or that Amber, their only healer, lay unconscious.

Stuart rested his hands over Amber. Minnett leaped on Amber's abdomen. Amber didn't move. Drew didn't believe she could move less if she were dead.

It took only a moment for Stuart to lean back. He put a hand on Minnett's back and closed his eyes.

Minnett's paws flexed like she was going to make biscuits

and touched Amber's belly. The cat half-closed her eyes. If Drew didn't know better, he'd think she was just a particularly happy cat sitting on her person.

She sat like that for several of Drew's breaths. He began to count his breaths, hoping to get a sense of the time that passed. He had just hit fifty-three when Stuart shook his head and removed his hand from Minnett's back.

Stuart took his time opening his eyes. Minnett was still sitting on Amber as if she'd changed from flesh and blood to stone.

"What's happening?" Drew thought to Mack. Stuart's eyes were opened but he hadn't raised his head. If he was still connected or offering energy to Minnett, Drew didn't want to interrupt him. Clearly whatever had happened was bad enough that neither of them was telling him to move Amber to her room. They were healing there, in Courtney's room, where Courtney slept, perhaps able to psychically attack even while she was unconscious.

"Minnett is healing Amber. Amber's energy is sluggish and feels cold. Her heart and mind were particularly impacted," Mack said. "I do not have more information as Minnett is not available to explain it to us."

"Can I do anything?" Drew asked.

"I believe Kayley is bringing up some food to Amber's room. Stuart, Amber, and Minnett will all need to eat after this, though I am uncertain if Amber will immediately wake. I would see if you are needed to carry Amber to her room when Minnett finishes."

Stuart finally lifted his head. He put a hand out towards the bed as if steadying himself, though he touched nothing. Then he looked up and around.

Drew glared at him.

"Minnett has things well in hand," Stuart said. "She should be finishing her healing shortly. Then it's probably best if you take Amber to her room."

Drew nodded. "What happened?"

"You probably know as much as I do from your bond-mate. All I know is that when we began to exit Courtney's energetic field, Amber wasn't with us. I felt as if she might have been in pain," Stuart said.

Drew didn't understand half of what Stuart told him but he didn't ask for clarity. Maybe later he'd ask Mack for assistance. Instead, he waited for Minnett to finish, which she finally did. The cat appeared wobbly and her fur stood too high.

Stuart picked her up and left the room, not waiting on Drew. Drew lifted Amber and carried her out the door, carefully angling so that she didn't bump her head against the jam. Julia was standing up, waiting. He heard her close the door behind him, softly with just the tiniest latch click.

The sound of voices reached him. Too far away to make out actual words, Drew had to settle for analyzing the emotions behind them. Someone, probably Tenny, sounded angry. Which meant Chase's involvement. Tenny rarely sounded angry with anyone except Chase. He made his way slowly down the stairs to the second floor, the voices getting louder, but no clearer.

Drew wondered if Chase had something to do with what happened upstairs.

The second floor was brighter than the third, the hall wider, which meant he could walk faster. Drew appreciated that because his arms were tiring. Naturally, Amber had the room at the end of the hallway.

Arriving there, he set her down on the bed as carefully as his tired arms would allow. Kayley was already there. She placed a dish of food for Minnett on the floor as Stuart set the cat down. Minnett wasted no time eating.

On the low dresser near the window, Kayley had placed some fruit slices as well as some cheese and crackers. A big bag of M&Ms lay off to the side, unopened. A glass of orange juice sat on a paper towel on that dresser and another sat on a napkin on the nightstand next to the bed where Drew had put Amber.

"We just need to let her sleep, now," Stuart said. "Unless Minnett is saying otherwise."

"She's not suggesting anything else," Mack informed Drew. *"She's busy eating. She thinks she's repaired the damage to Amber's energetic heart fields and her general body. If Amber doesn't wake in an hour, Minette will examine her again and see if she missed anything."*

Stuart wolfed down some cheese and gulped the orange juice before leaving the room. Kayley followed. She gave Drew a look and a nod of her head. Drew followed her back down to the front room. Cari was in the great room with Tenny who still had her arms crossed in front of her, her face hard and angry.

He heard people walking down the basement stairs, probably Matt and Chase.

Drew looked at the two women. Kayley shook her head. She settled in the chair near the darkened window. Drew took the chair next to her, wondering what she might want to talk about. She waited until Tenny stomped up the stairs before speaking.

COURTNEY

ourtney wandered in a field of dying red flowers. She recognized the place. She'd been there before she'd woken up trying to beat the shit out of her neighbor's car. Courtney's interest in flowers ran only to common flowers like carnations, roses, and tulips. She didn't recognize the red flowers, the five petals as smooth as velvet, some of which looked a darker red than others.

Looking down, Courtney intended to gauge how high they came on her legs, but she had no legs. She went to touch her face but felt no hand against her cheek. She couldn't see or feel any body parts.

Fear leached through her. She might not have a physical body, but she felt the emotion of fear, somehow. She clearly didn't understand the rules of this field of dying flowers or her part in it.

It occurred to her that she was dead or dying. Oddly, that didn't scare her so much as not understanding her surroundings.

She smelled nothing, but that would be normal if she had

no nose. She heard nothing, either, not even the faint trace of wind against the stalks of brownish-green. That, too, would be normal if she had no ears. Of course, the stalks didn't move, either, so perhaps the place was as wind-less as she was ear-less.

Yet she could see. Courtney wondered if that meant she had eyes. Or was sight such a major sense that her mind was making up something even though she was isolated in the dark, alone? The idea of not being able to trust her sight sent another tendril of fear racing through her.

That fear brought up another terror. While stuck in that field, her body might be running amok, murdering people with knives, or worse, and she'd wake with blood on her hands. Perhaps the dying flowers, with their dark red, almost blood-colored heads represented people she killed.

Courtney wasn't certain she'd only beaten her neighbor's truck. He had a dog. Maybe she'd murdered the dog. Or his son, though Courtney hoped the fact that she hadn't seen the boy meant he was safe with his mother who lived in another part of town.

The flowers raised their heads slightly as she wallowed in her emotions. Driving the terror back, Courtney concentrated on what she did know. She looked down at the flowers as if she were standing in a field. They might come up to her knees, if she had knees.

The stalks of the flowers were a sort of mottled brown and green, some with more green, others with more brown. Some of the flowers were brighter. Others had started to turn brown, their edges curled.

Nothing moved. Not a single flower changed position as she studied them.

Nothing changed in that place in which Courtney was trapped. If nothing changed, no one would save her. She would have to save herself.

Courtney thought back to everything her father told her about herself. A helpless child grown to a helpless adult. Her need for assistance, for company, was a failing that he'd never let her forget. His insistence upon her own self-reliance often bordered on abusive.

Perhaps he understood that there were places like the field of dying flowers where Courtney would need to rescue herself. As her father was not particularly given to mystical ideas, Courtney found that difficult to believe, but all the same, there she was. In this place. Alone but for the memories of his admonishments and suggestions.

She needed a body. Without legs to move her, she had no way of exiting the field.

First, Courtney needed to figure out how to get back to her body. She imagined her legs and feet and arms. She tried to think about what she saw in the mirror when she examined her breasts and her belly and even the way she turned to see her hips and her butt. She focused on feeling those things.

She recalled the heaviness of her legs after swimming in the lake with Hannah. She tried to imagine the sun on her back as they laid out near the lake, the warmth flooding through her skin and into her chest and down to her belly. Courtney thought about how the sweat that trickled along her hairline felt on those same lazy days.

She thought she heard something click on and felt warm air on her.

Excitement filled her.

She thought about flexing her fingers. She felt them doing exactly that.

Courtney bit down on her hope. She didn't want to be disappointed.

She brought her hands up to her face but saw nothing. Courtney struggled to open her eyes. Her fingers covered part of her face. Her hands were covered in a faint sheen of sweat.

Moving her hand, Courtney took in her surroundings. She lay in the same room she'd taken earlier, the teal and white of the day bed fluffed around her. Her stuff was unmoved. Her head rested on the daybed pillow she'd use later that night. It smelled faintly of cat and cat litter but Courtney doubted anyone else in the house would ever notice the scent.

She swung her legs off the edge of the bed, a slight headache threatening at her temples. Nothing too bad, just a sense that all was not quite right. Her stomach growled as if she'd not eaten anything in a very long time.

Courtney stood slowly. Her legs held her. She walked across the room, which was not that deep or that large. She should have asked for a bigger room when she asked to be confined. Not that she cared that much. She was just thankful to have her body back, though she dreaded what she might find outside the door. At least she didn't have literal blood on her hands.

Courtney opened the door, not surprised to find Julia there. Julia practically flew to her feet from her sitting position when Courtney saw her.

"What do you want?" Julia demanded.

Courtney had planned to ask for food. The hostility directed at her told her something had happened. She remembered being seated on the bed before she'd laid down. She didn't actually remember laying down or anything else.

"What did I do?" Courtney asked in a small voice, hoping against hope that she hadn't killed anyone, worried even that she had killed one of the cats. She didn't even like cats, yet here she was, terrified of having harmed one. The idea of hurting someone or something made her consider running away to be on her own. Only for a moment though, simply because she had nowhere else to go.

Julia sighed and began to tell her what had gone on while Courtney had been trapped in the field of dying flowers.

After leaving Amber's room, Stuart went down to the kitchen and started searching through the refrigerator for more food. He heard voices murmuring in the front room. The speakers were so close that soon enough he made out words and the general discussion.

Cari sat at the table, looking outside. She spent equal amounts of time looking at her tablet and out the windows. The deck held perhaps two inches of snow already and more was coming down. Fog was settling in, making it difficult to see the trees at the far end edge of the lawn, never mind the lake.

Stuart quickly put together a sandwich and wolfed that down while making another. The mustard tickled his nostrils and was hot enough that it gave him an ache at the back of his head. He put less on the second sandwich.

It had been a long time since he needed to cook. Someone from the clowder house often made large pots of spaghetti or stew that everyone ate. On other nights they were all on their own. The freezer was stocked with all sorts of easy to heat and eat food along with frozen staples like vegetables and hamburger and chicken.

Stuart could use the frozen foods but he was less certain of his abilities with the meats. He could cook eggs though, and sausage and bacon. He grabbed a snack pack of carrot sticks and a large apple to go with this sandwich and sat down at the table with Cari.

Kayley and Drew talked in the other room. Kayley was talking softly to Drew about how helpful he was around the clowder house. Stuart remembered the feeling when his cat had been retired and he'd been at loose ends. There had been pleasure in extra relaxation time but also guilt as if he ought to be doing something. He and Stardust had spent time together, sharing thoughts. Stuart read books, giving Stardust a wider glimpse of the human world.

They'd discussed the literature he'd read. Stuart held onto some of the insights his cat had conveyed to him and periodically savored them. He didn't remember ever feeling useless so much as at loose ends. Stuart had always known something would come up for him. Maybe it was the time and place as much as his personality that led him to that belief.

Now, in theory, he would be useful by Drew's standards, yet here he was, hated by at least one member of the clowder and mistrusted by the others. He couldn't say he blamed them. He didn't trust Base Command either, but those were not thoughts he could share with anyone.

Stuart chewed on the carrot sticks, having finished his second sandwich. He was still tired, but the need for food was easing. He'd go up to his room and lie down for a bit.

Cari looked up from her tablet as he started eating a carrot. "I'm getting a report of rioting near downtown Lexington."

"Is there a reason?" Stuart asked. People all over were

protesting and it seemed to take just one person breaking a window to start an all-out riot.

"Nothing that I can see. There wasn't even a crowd to start," Cari said. "The reports say that several people were coming out of the parking lot of a hospital. They just stopped their cars and got out and started hitting people who were already there. The people fought back. Several other people who were passing by stopped their cars and started fighting as well. Lots of broken windows in both the hospital and the surrounding businesses."

Stuart chewed thoughtfully. The gray outside was darker. The day had passed too quickly for him to absorb everything that had happened. "Violence went up in the last snow, too, didn't it?"

He knew the answer. It had. Cari needed to come to the same conclusion.

"It did," she said. "Not like this. Three people have been killed so far. Last time there were only injuries, at least in fights, if I remember correctly. Two people died due to hypothermia. We lost some pets and wildlife, too. Plenty of plants were gone. Lots of injuries and maybe a death or two from car accidents."

Stuart nodded. "Were the car accidents really accidents?"

"No one said otherwise," Cari said. "I remember there were stories of people driving crazy, so maybe…"

"I think this is an escalation of something that began last time. Just like Courtney's ability to hurt Amber escalated from last time. The frost witches are stronger this time. I know everyone hoped that we'd wounded them when we treated Courtney and Chase, but I believe we only drove them back. They took this time to assess our abilities. They waited until they were stronger and now they know us better, too."

Cari bit her lip, looking out the window. She shuddered.

"I'm not sure what we do with that information, but it's something we need to take into account," Stuart said quietly. He finished the last of his food.

"Wheelie tells me Anastasia agrees with your assessment."

Anastasia was the researcher cat. Not all clowders got researchers. The fact that one had been chosen for this clowder suggested an intelligence about what might happen. Stuart didn't think the command cats were prescient, but perhaps they were, at least to an extent. Riley was an interesting bond-mate choice as well. Stuart hadn't spent much time with her, though you'd think they'd be natural allies. Riley tended to keep to herself.

Granted, she was older than most of the rest of the clowder and had probably gotten used to her own company as time passed. Still, he ought to talk to her more, learn what she knew, what she thought, those things she might not be writing down in the annals of the clowder library. It was easy to overlook her because she was slow and didn't often join in downstairs, her hips paining her, despite Amber's healing. Even Stuart's healing had done less than he'd hoped.

He resolved that a chat with Riley would be high on his list of things to do when he woke from a nap. Stuart pushed himself up from the table when Cari's cell phone rang.

He removed his plate from the table and went to the sink to wash it as Cari set down her tablet and picked up her phone. After hello, she was silent for a long time. Her face appeared to pale. Then she hung up without saying anything.

"Is something wrong?" Stuart asked. He'd not seen fear, not real fear on Cari's face before, but her eyes were strained and her skin color poor. The sour smell he associated with human fear reached him.

"My mom," Cari said. "She called to tell me I ought to kill myself, something she described it in great detail."

"When was the last time you spoke with your mom?" Stuart asked.

Cari shook her head. "Last week. She was fine. She knew not to go out in the snow…"

Stuart felt the skin on his forehead tighten while he thought. Cari's mother must have gone out for some reason. If she hadn't, that left the question of how she'd become infected.

"Maybe someone else forced her to go out," Stuart suggested.

Cari looked at him with large worried eyes. "Maybe? But…"

He nodded. "This is definitely escalating."

Drew sat with Kayley in the front room. Around them, he heard the sounds of people moving from room to room. Chase and Matt had gone back downstairs, probably to play more pool. Matt took it upon himself to do most of the work with Chase, figuring if he were going to be infected with whatever this was, he'd already been exposed when he'd been trapped outside in the first snow.

Drew appreciated what Matt was doing. He felt like he ought to spend time with Chase to keep other people from having to do so, but Chase made him uncomfortable. Besides, Chase always seemed to know what he was thinking. It was hard to deal with.

"You aren't cut out for healing, you know," Kayley said.

Drew frowned at her, not sure where she was going with the conversation.

"I worked as an EMT before Elmore and I bonded. I went to school with people learning to be EMTs and you aren't cut out for it. That's not a bad thing," Kayley said.

Drew felt his chest and stomach tightening. He'd thought

that maybe he'd see about studying medicine, had even considered talking to Kayley about being an EMT.

"You're sensitive. And you worry," Kayley said. "You don't believe in yourself enough. That's one thing you have to do if you're treating patients. But, you listen. I think if you wanted to consider something other than shelter work it would be social work. It suits you better than medicine."

"What brought this up?" Drew asked. He knew, though, deep down. Amber was annoyed with him when he'd been following her whenever she examined Chase or Matt, and now, Courtney. He knew his presence bothered her because she worried he'd try and send her energy again. Drew would, too, because helping was the most important thing.

"Watching you with Amber and Stuart. I know you don't like Stuart," Kayley craned her neck and lowered her voice upon seeing him in the other room with Cari. "No one really trusts him, you know. But, he's the best person to help Amber right now. Mack may be retired but with everything going on, we're going to need guardians. Both of you have experience that the rest of us don't have. We might not need you on the front lines, but that doesn't mean we don't need you to support us and guide us."

Drew had never considered that as the senior guardian the others might look to him for guidance. The clowder was usually based on equality, or as much equality as felines allowed. Now, though, they were facing a crisis. A big one. He could be a leader.

"I should think about the kinds of things we should do," Drew said slowly.

Kayley nodded.

"Are there cats watching upstairs?" Drew asked. He spoke out loud, though he was talking to Mack. Mack would know that, of course.

"Anastasia and I are in the library looking out the windows,"

Mack said. *"Wheelie is in the cat tree keeping an eye on the back. Some cars have passed the street in the front but none have slowed or stopped. We believe they are people from the neighborhood arriving home from work."*

Kayley smiled at him. "You do have a use. You've just been so busy trying to remain active that you haven't realized that there are other ways to help."

Drew nodded. He appreciated the words. Listening. Like social work. He'd look into that. Base Command could be good about paying for extra schooling if someone in the clowder learned something they wanted to follow up on. Briefly, he wondered where they got the money to pay for everything.

Standing, Drew decided he needed to go up and talk to Riley. She'd been holed up in the library for the last month. He'd see her at breakfast sometimes and then again at dinner but she'd rarely been down for television. She'd never down to the basement, though before, she would sometimes make the trek down. Her hips had been particularly bad with the colder weather, though, too.

Feeling better about himself, planning on doing the best job he could at leading the clowder—assuming anyone but Kayley would listen—Drew jogged up the stairs. He'd look in on Amber, too, after talking to Riley.

"The cats will listen to me," Mack assured him, *"as an extension, the humans will listen to you. We are just in need of a plan."*

Drew paused at the top of the stairs, smelling the old book smell that wafted from the library and listening to the sounds around him. Tenny was in her room, banging around. He wondered what had happened to make her so angry. Kayley's words that he listened came back to him.

Drew went down the hall to the left instead of going to the library. He passed the white door to Kayley's room that she'd decorated with a photo of Elmore. A little further down on the other side of the hallway was Tenny's room. Her door wasn't closed all the way. Drew lifted a hand and knocked softly. The door creaked open wider.

"What?" Tenny called.

"What's going on?" Drew asked. He stepped in when she opened the door wider. Tenny was shorter than he was and rail thin. She didn't look like a fighter, but she was one of the strongest people Drew knew. Her curly dark hair which had once hung in dreadlocks was now shorn so short you could see the dark skin of her skull through it. A creature had once grabbed the locks which had been tied up in a bandana during a fight. Tenny had gotten a good scrape from her wrist to her shoulder because of it. The only reason it hadn't been worse was due to a bit of luck and her bond-mate Boyd's magical ability to change size and attack. The locks had been gone within hours of her being released from Amber's medic room.

"Chase. What else?" Tenny asked. She stomped across the room to the gray and green loveseat. She had laid out her room a bit like one of the hotel rooms that were called mini-suites. Her bed was against the wall with the door and the loveseat positioned near the window, against the far wall with a small table in front of it. The wall to the left of the door held a dresser and a desk with a chair. An upholstered trunk rested at the foot of the bed.

"What'd he do now?" Drew asked. He pulled out the desk chair to face the loveseat. The black swivel chair was a little small for him but probably fit Tenny perfectly.

Tenny rolled her eyes. "When Courtney came in and he went upstairs to see her, we all hurried to keep him away from her. He told me that I was too stupid to be part of the clowder like all my people."

Drew waited. Tenny wasn't one to get upset about insults.

"It was like he didn't even see me anymore," Tenny said. "I was just an anonymous Black person he could insult."

Drew bit his lip, wishing he knew what to say. He was a big white guy. No one ever insulted him. He knew, intellectually, that insults like that would hurt Tenny but he didn't know what to say or do to help.

"It's getting worse," Tenny said. "That's what scares me. Even Chase is getting worse. This isn't the first time he's acted like I'm some random person. It's happened with Anson, too."

"When?" Drew asked. He wanted to ask what. Maybe that would help him figure out what Tenny needed to hear. Anson was another white guy, if not quite as big as Drew.

"A few days ago. It was a stupid thing, really, something about college dropouts being unable to hack it. Normally, Anson wouldn't care. You know, a lot of times Chase has been saying things that are personal to try and get under your skin, but this was more general like he was seeing us not as the people around him but as… I don't know… background?" Tenny left the last as a question.

"Like we're not real?" Drew asked, thinking about some of what he'd heard.

"That's it," Tenny said. "He was trying to play us as people but now it's more like we're not real to him. Like he's further away from us. Damn it. I *liked* Chase. A lot."

Drew wondered what about the 'a lot' comment. Of course, Chase had dated outside the clowder. He and Tenny had been friends. Probably just good friends.

"I feel like he's gone and I can break down and cry or I can stomp around and use it against this bitch of a frost witch," Tenny said. "I'd rather do the latter."

"We just don't know exactly what to do," Drew said quietly. "We've been waiting for Stuart to make suggestions. Maybe we have to think about how we can fight them. We have our cats. We know our strengths. Maybe we need to play to them."

"How?" Tenny asked.

"I'm supposed to be retired, but Kayley reminded me that Mack and I have seen a lot of creatures. Maybe we figure out the kinds of things that have worked for us before and be ready to use them?" Drew suggested.

"So just sit around waiting for them to come out?" Tenny snapped. "I'm tired of waiting. We knew this snow was coming. I know we didn't want to admit it, but everyone was waiting. Especially Stuart."

"He knew they weren't gone," Drew said. "This time they're stronger, or acting stronger. What if it's another bluff?"

Tenny gave him a look, half turning her head away.

"They use our minds against us. The neighbors who came here don't remember what they did. What if all the frost witches can do is use people against each other?"

"They hurt Amber."

"Via Courtney," Drew said. "The neighbors came at us like people. Even when we had to fight them off, they just used human ways of fighting and those that didn't know how to fight didn't suddenly figure it out. Only Courtney, and probably Chase, have any extra powers."

"What are you saying?" Tenny asked.

"We need to figure out how to get the things out of the two of them," Drew said.

"Amber's been trying," Tenny replied. "It's all she's talked about since the last snowfall."

"We have to set a timeframe for learning something before we send them back through the portal," Drew said. "Somewhere they can't return from."

"Kill them," Tenny said, her voice flat.

Drew nodded. "We all know that's a possibility, but no

one is talking about it. We need to set a plan for what needs to have happened, or not happened, and how long we want to try and fight them. I mean, we have no idea how this thing spreads. Maybe we should have sent them through as soon as we thought of frost witches."

"You know you're starting to scare me a little," Tenny said. "The Drew I know isn't about to sacrifice his friends."

"What if it's the only way to save my other friends?" Drew asked.

"Let me put this to you," Tenny said, leaning forward, "if it comes down to sending Chase through the portal to save the rest of us, can you push him through?"

Drew wasn't sure he knew the answer to that. To say he couldn't do it, meant he was talking about things he, himself, couldn't do. If he said he could, then he felt horrible that he could consign a man who had once been his friend to death, even though his friend was walking and talking and appeared to be alive.

"That's what I thought," Tenny said, leaning back. "I don't disagree that we need to make a timeline and a plan. But we also need to be real clear what sending Courtney and Chase through the portal means. It means they die. We need to know what that's going to do to us as a clowder, too. Can we live without ourselves if we give up one of our own?"

COURTNEY

Courtney listened to Julia about what had happened to Amber. Courtney had no memory of doing anything. She'd been in her field of dying flowers.

"I don't remember," Courtney said. "I was stuck in this field with flowers that were dying. I was trying to get out. I've been there before, when I hit my neighbor's car with a baseball bat…" she didn't add that she feared she might have beaten his dog as well. Hopefully not. Surely, she'd have stopped herself if she was trying to hurt a dog, wouldn't she?

Julia just nodded.

"Do you need to take notes or something?" Courtney asked.

"Riley does that," Julia said. "The cats have good memories and will tell her when she's got time to record it."

Courtney knew the cats were telepathic. She didn't know they'd remember everything she said. She avoided asking more questions because there were things she didn't really want to know about the cats.

Her stomach hurt. Anxiety fluttered its butterfly wings

through her abdomen as she worried about what had happened and what might yet happen.

"Can you guys kill me?" Courtney asked.

Julia blinked at her, her mouth opened and then closed.

"I don't know how to stop this. I think you need to kill me." There she'd said it. Asked for it. Her throat felt tight. Tears lingered behind her eyes. She didn't want to die. She wanted to meet the right man, get married, have a family. She wanted her sister's life, really. Payton always seemed so content and eager for each day whereas Courtney often felt tired and dragged herself into work.

If she died now, she'd never have done anything worthwhile. What kind of mark does an insurance biller make? Certainly, she took pride in making sure the patients at the clinic were able to afford their medical care thanks to their insurance but she wasn't leaving much behind her. Not even a dog.

"We don't normally kill people," Julia said slowly as if she weren't sure how to respond.

"You can't let them examine me again. I don't really remember anyone coming in. I just remember the field and you say Amber got hurt, maybe badly," Courtney said. "I don't want to do that again but I don't know how to stop myself."

"We're working on ways to help you." Julia crossed her arms but one hand came up as if pushing Courtney further away from her.

Courtney nodded. She took the hint to go back into the room. She was still hungry. How long had it been since she'd eaten? Maybe the hunger would keep her from falling back into the field. If not, she'd use it as a punishment against herself for harming Amber.

Slipping back into the room, Courtney found her tablet. She'd been playing on it before she'd woken up. It sat safely out of the way on the window ledge. Curling up on the bed, in the same corner she'd sat in earlier, Courtney started searching out information on how to commit suicide, just in case.

Her internet hung and the little wheel on her tablet just kept spinning. Courtney frowned. She backed out and went back to playing her game, which did come up just fine. Obviously, the thing that inhabited her didn't want her to learn how to die. It would no doubt try and stop anyone from killing her, too.

Courtney sighed. Was she possessed? When she quit her game to research possession, her tablet worked just fine. Either the entity didn't care what she knew about possession, she wasn't actually possessed, or it didn't think regular information about possession would make any difference.

Of course, information on possession all talked about religion. If it came from a different world, through a portal, as the people at the clowder called them, then it wouldn't react to religious symbols. Or could it? Courtney turned that over in her mind. Didn't she read some vampire book where a vampire said the symbol was about the belief behind it? Maybe this was like that. Maybe it was the belief?

If she believed that a priest or a minister could cast out the entity, would that work?

Courtney started to feel cold. She moved around and pulled the daybed covers around her shoulders. Still, the longer she read, the more she shivered. She got out of bed and went to the door.

Julia stood waiting by the door, ready for anything. No doubt she heard Courtney moving.

"Is it cold in here?" Courtney asked. She didn't see her breath but her body was chilled. She shivered as she stood, crossing her arms and bouncing while she waited the intermittent time for Julia to answer.

"Not really," she said. Julia looked her over. "I can have someone bring up some cocoa or something?"

"That would be good. I've been hungry." Courtney didn't want to whine but maybe her chills were due to a lack of food.

Julia gave her a half-smile as her eyes went slightly unfocused. Probably communicating with the cat.

Courtney closed the door softly and hurried back to her daybed, shivering. She was too cold to play on the tablet. Her fingers felt stiff. She huddled and shivered under the blankets, her knees up to her chin and arms cradled close. She breathed down into the covers, hoping that whatever warmth she got from her breath would help keep her body from freezing.

Courtney waited the longest time. She felt as if she could have gone to the store and purchased a hot chocolate three times over before anyone came upstairs with anything. A knock on the door.

"Come in!" Courtney yelled.

Tenny came in with a bag of food. "We don't have any trays, unfortunately," she apologized. She set the bag down near the wall, not getting too close to Courtney. She also set down a big mug of something steaming and a thermos.

"Thanks," Courtney said, her teeth chattering. Couldn't they come closer to her to warm her up?

"I heated up some potato skins and there's a sandwich in the bag. More hot chocolate in the thermos in case you need more to keep you warm. I heated the chicken in the sandwich before I brought it up," Tenny explained.

"Thanks," Courtney muttered again, her teeth chattering so hard she could barely talk.

"I'll try and find another heater." Tenny left the room, leaving Courtney to decide between sitting beneath the covers with her teeth chattering or getting up, out of the covers to grab the food.

Her stomach growled.

The people in the house were cruel. It wasn't that they didn't want to kill her, they wanted her to suffer! Here she was, freezing practically to death in their house and they put food in a corner half a room away from her. Who did that?

The anger, as it often did, warmed Courtney. Her teeth stopped chattering and though chilled, she made her way to the food and the hot drink. She ate the sandwich quickly but saved the potato skins to savor while she worked on her tablet. The hot chocolate warmed her insides further.

Courtney closed her eyes savoring the heat as she settled back to work on the tablet. She wondered if the entity had made her so cold so she couldn't look anything more up.

*A*mber hurt. Pain stabbed through her head, still, like someone had shoved an icepick through the top of it and threaded it down to the base of her skull. No matter how she turned, she couldn't find any real relief.

It felt like a band was wrapped around her chest. It ached every time she took in a deep breath, which also set off the pain in her head once again.

"You were very injured," Minnett said through their telepathic link. *"I can try and relieve the pain if you like."*

"Please," Amber said. She felt Minnett's surprise followed quickly by concern. Amber didn't often ask for assistance in healing. Normally, she'd have gotten up and gotten her acupuncture needles and given herself a treatment. The pain was bad enough that she didn't think she could move.

Her stomach growled but at the same time, the idea of food made her nauseous.

Minnett settled in with her front paws on Amber's belly. Amber followed Minnett through their telepathic link so she could see what had happened to her body on the energetic level.

The energy around her heart was weak, a pale image of what it should be. Minnett had wrapped a sort of energetic bandage around her chest, which was the band that Amber felt. Looking through Minnett's eyes, she saw the energy still trying to leak out. The band needed to stay.

Warmth flooded her chest, though, as Minnett sent healing energy towards Amber's heart.

"What did it look like before?" Amber asked.

"On the physical level it was not bad," Minnett said. *"Your heart was still working but a little sluggish in the area where the energy was leaking out. The energetic level was worse. I wrapped it because the rip in your heart's energy was getting larger."*

Amber felt a chill go through her. Without heart energy, she might have gone on for several days, a shadow of herself without any real joy. Eventually, the low energy would have worked its way to a physical issue, a heart attack most likely.

The warmth made her chest feel less achy, though Minnett didn't loosen the band. Amber no longer saw energy leaking but apparently, Minnett felt it was too soon to relieve the pressure.

They moved up into Amber's head. There, she saw energetic tears all over the center area of her mind. Energy didn't leak from her mind so much as it appeared frozen. Again, Minnett began to warm her Amber's head. The heat soothed the pain and Amber breathed more easily.

Minnett backed off while Amber continued to lie back in bed. The pain returned, but the intensity was not as great. Food wasn't going to turn her stomach. Neither was standing up to get to the food to feed herself.

"Thank you," Amber said aloud to Minnett.

"It was a lot of healing," Minnett said. *"I would love another can of food."*

"Tell someone who can bring some up that I said it was okay," Amber said. While she wouldn't put it past most cats to try to get more cat food, the telepathic bond meant that lying was difficult.

The table held cheese and orange juice. Amber gulped down the fruit juice, knowing the easy sugar would rebuild her energy more quickly. Then she gobbled down the food. There was a feast there, enough to have held her most of an afternoon on a normal day. Instead, it left feeling as if she'd had a light snack after a famine.

She should have asked Minnett to have someone bring up food for her, too.

"I suggested it," Minnett said. "Stuart was ravenous when he finished checking you over to be sure Courtney had not infected you."

"Did she?" Amber asked, her chest clenching even tighter while she worried that she'd done something to endanger Minnett. If she were infected, they hadn't determined whether the infection could reach the cats through the telepathic bond.

"Not so far as Stuart and I can tell. Your energy patterns remain consistent, despite the pain. Granted you are losing energy, however, there isn't anything new in your patterns. I see no darkness. My impression was that Courtney attempted to hurt you more than infect you," Minnett said.

Amber sat back down on the bed, tired again after eating, though the food only reminded her of how ravenous she really was. Someone knocked on the door.

"Come in!" Amber called. She ought to have gotten up and answered but her legs felt heavy and her head was beginning to hurt again. The pain was a diffuse ache along with the stabbing pain that came perhaps twice every minute.

Tom came through the door. "We need trays. Tenny's preparing some food for Courtney, too. All we have are bags."

Tom carried two beige plastic bags from their local

grocer. Amber saw containers with a sandwich, crackers and cheese, chocolate, and another steaming container of something hot.

"What's the hot item?" Amber asked as Tom set the food down. She stood up, moving slowly and carefully to the dresser.

"Poppers. I know you like them. I put in some carrots and jicama sticks for you, too. I can heat soup if you want that."

"Soup would be good but the heavier food is probably better. Put me back to sleep," Amber said, trying to keep it light.

The second bag had less in it, but it was a can of food and a spoon to dish it up for Minnett. The cat ate eagerly, beginning to chow down as soon as the food was in front of her. While Minnett, like most cats, hated to miss a second of eating, she was normally more polite.

Amber didn't feel any less ravenous and began on the carrot sticks. Tom had added in a small dish of ranch dressing. Amber coated the sticks with the dressing, hoping it would be enough.

"Do you need me to stay?" Tom asked.

"I'm good," Amber said. "Thanks."

Tom nodded. He had barely left the room when someone else knocked.

"Come in!" Amber called, her mouth still partly full.

Drew stuck his head in. "I wanted to make sure you didn't need anything."

"Tom brought plenty of food. I'll nap after, I think," Amber said.

Drew nodded. He stood awkwardly in the doorway, acting unsure of what to do. Amber didn't have the energy to deal with him. She kept eating, hoping he'd figure out what he wanted to say.

A sudden crash. The sound of glass shattering reached Amber. Downstairs. Something had happened.

Drew said not a word but turned and ran for the stairs.

"Stay here," Minnett ordered. *"Two people from the neighborhood have broken in the sliding door on the deck."*

It wasn't lost on Amber that they hadn't gone through the windows on the basement, where Chase was. Adrenaline surged through her body as she prepared herself for this new threat.

STUART

Stuart sat up as if he'd never been asleep, every alarm in his body chiming. The hair on the back of his neck raised and he knew something was wrong. He heard running feet and yelling.

Stuart's body flowed upwards and he hurried out the door. He rubbed his left eye while leaving the room, then wiped what felt like a bit of dried spittle at the corner of his mouth. He'd slept more deeply than he had since he'd been called to Lexington. He'd probably overused his abilities when working with Amber.

Julia was on her feet, leaning forward, but she stayed at Courtney's door. Good. They needed people there.

At the landing on the second floor, Riley was at the door. Several of the cats had gathered in the library. No one followed him to the first floor. Stuart was the last one heading down. He'd really slept far too hard.

He kept a hand on the round pale pine knob that made up the end of the banister as he swung himself around. The front room was empty but for long gray shadowy furniture. Kayley had left her post.

The great room behind it, however, was another story. Fin, Tom, Tenny, Cari, and Kayley were all in there. Tom and Fin pushed people out the door. Tenny had a huge board that she was attempting to push towards the window. Cari was helping her.

Stuart focused his energy. He grounded his body, letting some of his energy reach down to the earth beneath the house. When he felt that connection, that energy running through him, he pushed it outward, creating a shield of sorts. First Fin and then Tom drove the attackers through the broken glass of the door, careful to stay inside the house, barely letting a hand go out.

The attackers attempted to get back in, but Stuart's shield kept them out. He felt the edges of the shield begin to fray, forcing him to draw more energy to keep the shielding in place. Mentally, he formed a sort of dome of protection around the entire clowder house, including the basement below.

Stuart was only vaguely aware of Tom helping Tenny and Cari get the board in place. The sound of a hammer pounding nails reached him though it took him a moment to find Kayley using the hammer to keep the plywood in place.

Fin brushed Stuart's arm as he hurried to the basement.

Stuart let his senses seek out other dangers. Downstairs he felt only a thick darkness. He had to search for Matt and Anson, both of whom were down there, alive. Stuart couldn't look deeper to check patterns and still hold the shield.

"Wheelie says the cats have it," Cari called.

She hadn't used his name but Stuart knew she was talking to him. He let his magic go and hurried downstairs. It was almost a shock that the main room in the basement was as bright as it was. The lights were on inside and with the white snow outside light permeated most corners, despite the failing sun. The glass on those windows remained untouched.

Chase held a pool cue and stared at the table. Matt was looking out the window. Anson stood next to him, turned so that he could see both the outside and keep an eye on Chase. Fin stood near the door.

"I could get an umbrella," Fin said. "Pull the hurricane shutters here."

"Add ski gear," Stuart said. "Double up on gloves and make sure anything you wear is waterproof."

"I can do it," Anson said. "We had to get back from the park in this." Stuart noticed the tiredness about Anson, then. He was in sweats and socks. He, too, must have been awakened when the people broke in.

Chase said nothing. He kept looking at the pool table, searching for a shot. Stuart noted three shots. Two would put in striped balls. One would put in the orange five in the side pocket. Chase ignored that one. Stuart wondered what game he was playing or if he was paying more attention to the others than he wanted them to know.

Stuart wondered about all the pool playing. He looked up at the flat ceiling which was higher than he'd expect in a basement but not so high as the first-floor ceiling. Painted in flat cream paint, Stuart noted nothing about it that would give anything away. He let his focus soften and he looked at it through energetic eyes.

Coming through the overhead light, a stained-glass fixture patterned with cats, was a pale white energy. It floated down like the snow outside, but it unfailingly landed on Chase.

As if he knew what Stuart was doing, Chase looked up at him and smiled. Then he went back to studying the table.

Stuart let go of the vision. Part of him wanted to shake Chase but he didn't know what would happen if he did.

Everything was an unknown. Right now, they needed to learn about the creatures they faced. It would do them no good to react too strongly.

Anson appeared in the time that Stuart had been looking at the energy. Anson now wore ski pants and a heavy jacket. His hood was up and he had on a hat under that.

"Are the people still up on deck?" Anson asked.

"I thought I saw them leave the deck and go back around front," Fin said. "Can't be sure."

"Anastasia said she watched two men walking down our driveway," Matt said quietly.

Anson raised his eyebrows and went outside, carrying an umbrella which he set carefully near one of the deck supports. The entire window was beneath the deck. It was easy enough to close the hurricane shutters down there. They probably should have done so earlier, but it hadn't seemed worth even the minor risk of getting hit with the snow. Anson couldn't use the umbrella. He needed both hands for the shutters.

Stuart noted that the snow fell harder while he was out there. Fortunately, they'd all practiced opening and closing the shutters so it didn't take long to close them. Anson would then need to walk around the house, under the dubious protection of the umbrella to get inside. Climbing the stairs to the main house wasn't an option.

The room was darker now, more cave-like

Stuart watched Chase continuing to survey the pool table, not finding a shot. Looking at him again, Stuart noted that the energy was no longer flowing into him. Still, Chase seemed to be concentrating on something else. Stuart wished he knew what it was.

$\mathcal{A}$fter eating Courtney felt stronger. A brief rush of energy, like a second wind, reached her perhaps half an hour later. She sat up, wondering why she felt so good.

She hesitated to go to the door, not sure what Julia knew. Even if Julia did know what had happened—and Courtney was certain something had—she could think of no reason Julia would tell her.

Instead, she pulled out her tablet and went back to searching for information. When she'd decided that it might be belief that made something work, she'd gotten cold. The entity, then, not only knew what she was thinking, it understood.

Of course, it took over her body at will. Mostly. Courtney frowned, wondering if she had been doing or not doing something in particular when the entity took over. When it had sent her to the field of dying flowers and she'd attacked Amber, she would have been relaxing. Amber would have been examining her.

When she'd attacked her neighbor's truck, she'd been

sitting on the sofa, watching television, having a snack. Also relaxing.

If she remained vigilant, perhaps she could fight the entity off. It would also require she remain awake for long periods of time. Not only that, she'd need to remain attentive while she remained awake.

Courtney remembered the cold chill she'd gotten when she found the information about belief. Maybe that was the entity feeding off her body heat. Like a vampire. Except instead of coming from the outside, this vampire was already inside her. Courtney wondered if it could feed on others while inside her or if it needed her to do something to them.

The idea that the entity was a sort of vampire felt strangely comforting. Courtney was a huge fan of vampire books, movies, and television shows. In fact, the only vampire novel she wasn't that keen on was the scary one by Stephen King, but that was old and those vampires were mean.

The entity inside her didn't seem to be very nice, though, which meant she couldn't count on a sudden romantic attraction to help her. Besides, that would be weird. She'd be in love with herself.

Courtney bit her lip, thinking of everything she knew about vampires. Most books said garlic was bad, though many of the nicer vampires had no problems with it. They also didn't like sunlight. Clouds followed these entities around, so perhaps they, too, disliked the brightness of the sun.

Amber and the others at the clowder had called them Frost Witches and suggested that they fed on the life of worlds and people. Apparently, legends held that they even ate suns. That didn't make sense if they didn't like the light.

Or maybe they didn't like the light until the worlds were mostly dead and there was nothing else to feed on. Courtney started making notes on her tablet. She saved frequently and even made a backup under a different name. In case the entity took over and tried to delete the notes.

Courtney started to feel cold, again. The chill started in her belly and quickly moved to her hands and feet. It became uncomfortable to hold the tablet. Courtney pulled the blanket around her more closely.

Above her, the furnace clicked on. The heat blew down on her but it wasn't nearly warm enough for Courtney. The entity definitely did not like what she was learning. Courtney didn't know how far it would push her body. So far, it didn't want her dead. It wanted her submissive.

Her friend, Hannah would be great at getting rid of the darned entity if all she had to do was remain in control and in charge. Hannah was good at that. Payton, too, had a take-charge attitude. Courtney let life happen to her. She let her father tell her what to do. She let him chose where she lived, for heaven's sake!

The self-flagellation warmed her slightly. She couldn't get distracted though. She needed to figure out how she could fight. Taking stock of things that might be strengths, Courtney knew she could run reasonably fast. Payton said she was sneaky. Not wanting to be confrontational, Courtney learned how to get what she wanted by getting around her parents rather than arguing with them. She'd make a decent spy.

She would not make a decent strong-woman.

Unfortunately, she was going to need to learn to be strong if she were to survive.

Courtney shivered under the blanket, putting aside the tablet for now. No sense in wearing herself down before she had a plan. Her eyes drifted shut and before she knew it, she was back in the field of dying flowers.

The field wasn't cold. In fact, there, Courtney didn't feel

her body at all, not the hunger that had been growing in her, not the cold. Of course, she couldn't feel herself breathing nor could she feel the flowers rubbing against her legs. She didn't even have legs when she was in the field.

Courtney focused on her body. That had worked last time. She thought about the way it hurt when she laid on her left side and put her arm under her pillow. Her shoulder always felt twisted in that position. She didn't feel that way when she slept on her right side. Just her left.

She focused on the pain. She focused on the way the shivering felt as she sat under the blanket.

It felt real. She smelled hot chocolate and potato skins. Courtney thought hard about opening her eyes. At first, there was nothing there to open. Then, gradually she began to feel as if she had eyelids that could move, though they felt heavy. Finally, she was able to open her eyes. She was still on the daybed. The entity hadn't sent her out to murder anyone. At least she hoped not.

Though still cold, Courtney left the bed to look out, opening the door barely a crack, afraid of what she might see.

She breathed out in relief when she saw Julia standing up, near the wall, clearly on guard but unhurt.

"Yes?" Julia asked.

"I fell asleep," Courtney said. "I wanted to make sure I didn't hurt anyone again."

Julia shook her head. "You'd know if you tried, believe me."

Courtney didn't smile but closed the door. She leaned back against it. How could she remain vigilant when she was already so tired?

DREW

It had taken more time than Drew liked to pull out plywood from the garage. He'd sent Tenny back with a sheet for the broken glass door in the great room but he wanted some for the smaller bedroom windows in the basement and first floor. Chase's room had the shutters closed but they were still open on Anson and Matt's rooms.

Upstairs, the whole room felt open and sunny. Too bad they hadn't had enough warning to close the shutters back there. Fin's room would need a board, but Drew's was beyond the reach of the deck. The unused front bedroom was also a potential access point.

Drew sneezed once. Sawdust and general dust from moving everything around. He'd put the boards where he had thought they'd be easy to reach but other large quantities of staples had been set in front of the plywood. Proving that he was the only one who believed they'd need to use the boards.

Stuart might have thought the frost witch wasn't gone, but Drew figured Stuart either didn't bother with supplies and accessibility, or else he had some hope that they could close the shutters before the snow started. Drew had no idea how anyone was supposed to know when a big storm was about to start.

Snow had fallen before in fits and spurts, a quarter-inch here and there, enough to keep small mounds in the shadows of side yards and bushes, but not enough to cause problems. Today the snow was falling harder and longer. Perhaps smaller, less intense snowfalls didn't enable the frost witches to control people.

Drew groaned slightly as he picked up three large plywood boards to take downstairs. The boards were tall and wide and the shape made them as difficult to move as their weight. At least the door between the house and garage could be left open. The cats knew better than to go out and not let someone know. Today, they wouldn't go out at all, staying towards the center of the house, offering their magical support rather than physical support.

Drew heard the sounds of hammering as Kayley and Tom finished covering the big broken window upstairs.

Tom came and tried to take the sheets of plywood for the rest of the windows.

"I was going downstairs with these, for Anson and Matt," Drew said.

"Probably only need one for each room," Tom said, taking one anyway.

Tom annoyed Drew by not listening to him. He might have been right but why couldn't they at least pretend. They'd not listened when he said the plywood could be important if they couldn't get outside. Instead of making sure there was easy access, someone had piled cases of cat food around the sheets of wood, causing one to warp slightly.

Instead of arguing, Drew let Tom take one of the large boards. The great room was already darker. The hammering stopped, for the moment, but it began again when Drew started down the stairs. The basement stairs hadn't been built to carry large items down. The side yard was wide and the doors down there could easily have accommodated most furniture. No one expected that there might be a day when it wasn't safe to use that access.

It made Drew's journey slow. Stuart waited at the bottom, looking up. He didn't offer to help. He backed up when Drew reached the bottom of the staircase and it was obvious that Drew was going to have to make an awkward turn, setting the sheets down and pivoting them around, one at a time, scraping the ceiling.

Matt came to help Drew carry them down the hallway, leaving Chase at the pool table. Anson was nowhere around. Mack had told him Anson was drawing the shutters. It took Drew a moment to realize that Anson would then have had to go around the house to come inside.

"If there's a fire while we're in here, that's going to be a problem," Drew said.

"The shutters will open from the inside if we need them to," Matt said. He took one of the sheets of plywood and carried it to his room at the far end. Drew carried his to Anson's and set it near the wall. He needed to go back up to get nails and a hammer.

"You think that'll work?" Chase asked when Drew reached the main room again. Stuart was gone. Chase was alone for the moment.

"What?" Drew asked.

"The wood?" Chase walked around the pool table again, not looking at Drew. He might have been talking to the eight ball for all the attention he gave Drew.

"Sure," Drew said. "We'll cover the windows from the inside. It should be about as good as the shutters outside."

"I'm already inside," Chase said, smiling. Then he lined up

a shot and took it, scattering the balls, sending three of them into pockets. The shot impressed Drew. More Matt's style than Chase's, really.

Chase looked at Drew and smiled. "Like everything you do, this is useless."

Drew grit his teeth to keep from saying something he'd regret and went upstairs.

Stuart climbed the stairs slowly. Chase had changed in the last day. Before, he hadn't been trusted, had played on that to annoy the rest of the clowder from time to time. He made a big deal of taking meals downstairs so as not to disturb people. Of course, while preparing his meal to go downstairs, Chase did all he could to annoy everyone else in the kitchen. But that was as far as it went.

Chase, Matt, Drew, and sometimes Anson or Fin would play pool downstairs for hours. Stuart knew that in between times, Chase read while Matt or Anson watched television on the small television that hung on the back wall of the room with the pool table.

Today, though, today…

Chase was up to something. Stuart couldn't put his finger on what it was. Before, Chase's actions were those of a pissed off teenager. The actions today were those of a watchful soldier, just waiting for a signal.

The signal wasn't the snowfall, though. That had started. It might, however, be a first sign, rather like the clandestine phone call with a voice that just says, "It's on." Now Chase was waiting for another signal, one that told him to make his move.

Sundown was coming. Would the witches be more powerful after dark? Or was there something else yet to come? The clowder had stopped the break-in through the glass window too easily. Something else was coming.

The main room was darker with the plywood. Tom held another board against the window and Tenny was pounding in nails to hold that one up in case that glass was broken. The breakfast alcove with the three large windows still needed boards.

Stuart turned when Anson came in through the front door. Anson pulled his key from the lock and finished shaking off snow around his boots. The trail of snow on the porch suggested that he'd already been shaking off the snow that landed on him earlier.

"Okay?" Stuart asked. He tuned into his energetic vision, what others might call psychic vision, and watched as Anson answered. There were no changes in his energetic patterns. Chase's patterns changed from day to day. Unfortunately, Stuart hadn't known Chase before he was infected so didn't know if perhaps one day he was seeing the patterns of the real Chase and another those of the frost witch. Patterns existed everywhere. Stuart doubted that the frost witch patterns in a human's energetic field could vary too much from person to person.

"Other than freezing my ass off out there, fine," Anson said. "No wind, so the umbrella protected me."

Stuart nodded and turned to go up the stairs to the second floor. He had been wanting to talk with Riley. As he climbed the stairs the hairs on the back of his neck raised. He smelled something burnt, which was one of his warnings that magic was being used.

He sniffed again but the scent was gone. Still, an energy

wrapped his body. The stairs felt taller than they should have, similar to the dreams Stuart had had where stairs never seemed to end. Stuart closed his eyes for a moment. Mentally he ascertained he was not dreaming. He actually was climbing stairs to the second floor of the clowder house.

With his eyes closed, he searched for where the sense of magic came from.

Above him. Courtney.

Perhaps there would be a designated time that she and Chase would meet and combine their powers. He ought to rest. Of course, he also needed to learn more. They needed more time to search through old records, old legends, at Base Command and Cat Home.

Darla, his boss at Base Command told him that the legends were ancient. While Cat Home kept excellent records, these weren't exactly easy to access. No one had done so, not in living memory.

While just one galaxy was vast beyond imagining and one universe was larger than that, multiple universes became unfathomable even to Stuart's mind. The idea that the frost witches had been encountered and then disappeared for ages was difficult to believe. Stuart wondered what had happened to them.

The endless walk to the second floor finished. The dreamlike quality disappeared, though he still felt a vague energy in the house that hadn't existed before. He found it difficult to describe. It was akin to walking into a house and knowing it was empty when one expected to find people.

Stuart walked through the door to the library. The calico cat, Anastasia, sat on the blue cushions that lined the lower shelves beneath the windows and watched the front of the house. Drew's big orange tabby, Mack sat with her, though Mack had turned to keep an eye on Stuart as he came into the room.

Mack yawned as Stuart passed. From the far end of the room, Stuart heard the squeak of an office chair. Anastasia had let Riley know he was there.

The clowder researcher was past middle age, her hair starting to gray. She walked slowly, with hips that were painful and sore. A solid woman, she wore black fleece sweatpants and black slippers embroidered with calico cats. She was the least prepared to go outside if need be, but she and Amber would be the last to fight.

"Can I help you?" Riley asked. Her voice had the slightest Southern twang. Her neck jutted forward as if to challenge him.

"Checking in," Stuart said. He gestured to her to go back to her desk. Riley turned, waddling back, though ducks made waddling look easy and whatever it was Riley was doing did not look easy at all.

Riley sighed as she sat. So did the chair. Stuart couldn't be certain but it looked like it sank a millimeter upon her settling in.

He pulled another chair from a desk a few rows up. Riley liked to hide in the back corner of the library. Books were scattered across the desk. The pale wood shelves had books falling sideways and bright green placeholders peppered the room like weeds in a garden. Leaning forward, Stuart noticed two large piles under the desk as well as the books scattered across it. Riley probably had just as many in her room across the hall.

"Haven't found anything new," Riley said.

"I didn't expect so," Stuart told her. "Cat Home hasn't come up with anything. I'm wondering more about the people here. What makes Chase different?"

"What do you mean?" Riley gave nothing away. Her first cat, Louisa, had been a healer. Riley had stayed at the clowder after Louisa had died and another cat had taken over. There had, in fact, been two healer cats between Riley's Louisa and Amber's Minnett.

"You've been here the longest. You know the people. To be a healer, you have to see people. You don't completely lose those talents. So you'd have sized up Chase when he came here. How is he different since the frost witches?"

Riley sighed. "I don't like to talk out of turn."

Stuart pretended to turn a little key on his lip. Probably an outdated gesture but it was so hard to keep up. He hoped Riley would just take it as one of his many eccentricities.

"Chase was always a good hunter. Made the most of himself, I think, and pretty proud of it. He tended towards practicality, liked his time alone," Riley said. She stopped and frowned. "Now, he plays pool. All the time. I think everyone else down there is sick of it. Matt joked that I needed to go down and take a pool shift. We don't even call it keeping an eye on Chase. It's all about playing pool with Chase."

"Did he just learn to play pool?" Stuart asked.

Riley shook her head. "He's always been up for a game or two but usually he'll end up in his room, listening to some music. He's always been sort of the watcher ideal. Loves alone time. A good observer. Now, all he seems to observe is the pool table. I see him around dinner when he makes a point of annoying everyone but that's it."

Stuart hadn't noticed anything unusual about the pool table. The only thing that seemed unusual was the energy coming down through the light. Above was the great room where everyone gathered. The clowder had been scared and angry when the energy had been flowing to Chase. The neighbors breaking in earlier had probably been equally scared.

He drummed his fingers on the edge of Riley's desk, though his knuckles hit the books. He stared off into the corner. Riley let him stare that way.

"Trag says that Chase was more irritable in the days leading up to the first snow. He feels as if Chase became more withdrawn from him. Not exactly secretive, but as if Chase was hiding something from him. The sense I get is what I remember from being a child when I knew my parents had hidden Christmas presents and they knew what was in them, but I didn't. It's not how Trag describes it but it's what I think of when I see what Anastasia translates for me."

Something hidden. Stuart wondered what it was.

"Trag would bond with you if you need," Riley said. "It would help you here. You'd have a direct link to our cats."

Stuart smiled. "That's generous of him…" he was going to suggest something else. Trag didn't need to know all of Base Command's secrets lest he re-bond with Chase.

"He said he's good with only a light bond. He won't know all your secrets," Riley said. "And he will only tell you Chase's, so you won't know all of his, either."

"It's a good idea," Stuart said. Trag would boost his own energy. Though with all that was going on, it would be easy enough for him to wear the cat out. He had no desire to do that.

Trag sauntered in the library as if this was the most normal thing in the world. When he got close to Stuart, Stuart felt the cat's mind telepathically knocking at the door of his own mind. In a normal human, there are no walls. Stuart opened himself up to Trag, or as much as he could, and then he was bound to the black cat.

His world opened up again to encompass another viewpoint. Another voice spoke to him in his mind. Stuart wasn't alone, as he'd been for decades, even surrounded by people who should have been trustworthy.

Just as he was relaxing into the feeling, the bond was gone. Perhaps Trag had seen something Stuart should have kept hidden. Stuart didn't even know how to ask. He looked up at Riley who had paled. Her face looked stricken as she reached out a hand to grab her desk. Maybe this wasn't about him at all.

COURTNEY

Courtney managed to walk across the room to the bed, where she flopped down on it, hanging on as if she worried that in her fatigue her body would flop to the floor no matter what she wanted. Her stomach felt rather ill like she'd not eaten in ages, although she'd just had food. She was cold but pulling the blanket up around her felt like too much work.

The field of dying flowers beckoned her. Closing her eyes, almost involuntarily, she saw the flowers. Knew then that if she fell asleep she'd be back in that field. Courtney struggled against it. Maybe if she asked for soda or coffee or even tea, the caffeine would wake her up. This fatigue, though, felt deeper than the fatigue of not having slept.

She felt as if someone had stolen all her energy. Now, she was a wrung-out rag. Courtney forced herself to sit up, struggling against the covers. The coldness, the fatigue had begun when she'd been thinking about the idea of belief and also vampires. Yes. Her lack of energy felt the way she thought she might feel after a vampire had sapped it.

Garlic warded against vampires. Also silver. She hadn't thought to bring any of her jewelry, not that she had anything that she thought was real silver. Daylight. Courtney glanced out the window with the open blind. The gray clouds were getting darker as the sun was setting. No hope there.

The room looked exponentially larger as Courtney thought about pushing herself up and walking to the door to ask for garlic. Lots of garlic. She fantasized about one of those large garlic wreaths to hang around her neck. If that didn't help, nothing would.

If she had the energy, she'd drive to the store and buy out all the garlic they had. It's not like the snow could hurt her. Unfortunately, she could barely keep her eyes open. The entity might not let her be hurt in an accident but Courtney didn't doubt that it wouldn't care about anyone else she might injure while driving.

Eyelids, drooping, she placed a hand on the wall and slowly walked back over to the door. The wall was warm against her palm. Courtney figured the floor would feel that way against her bare feet, though she had no intention of taking off her slippers. She was far too cold. As soon as she gave up control, she'd probably have energy.

Everyone always wanted her to give up her own control! Her father, for instance, was always telling her what to do, not caring about her wants. Chase had always chosen where to eat even when he knew Courtney didn't like the food at some restaurant. There was one BBQ place that had such fatty brisket it made her sick to her stomach every time they ate there, yet it was Chase's favorite and he'd drive them over to it anytime BBQ was suggested.

Courtney admitted they had good sauce, but the chicken was tough, the brisket fatty, and the pork not well shredded.

Even their coleslaw was dull and their sweet tea had only a passing acquaintance with sugar.

Courtney preferred a place over by her house that had better meat and a wider selection of sauces but Chase was loathe to go there. It wasn't his place. So they ate where he wanted.

When she went out with Hannah to the movies, Hannah always decided what movie to see and what bar to go to if they were having a girl's night. Mostly Courtney didn't mind, but would anyone ever let her make decisions about her life?

Payton always gave her judgmental opinion about Courtney's clothing choices and would have her dressing like a girl in her late teens in 1950 rather than a modern-day woman. Hannah was equally judgmental, but Hannah's judgments were about whether something showed off Courtney's breasts to effect, not too much, not too little cleavage. Courtney always messed up.

The anger she felt thinking about these wrongs, warmed her and gave her the energy to cross the room. Opening the door, this time with more confidence, Courtney looked out.

Julia was standing, waiting, a look of minor annoyance on her face. She'd probably just gotten comfortable again.

"Can I get some garlic?" Courtney asked.

"Garlic?" Julia repeated.

"As much as you can. You know, like one of those wreaths. I was thinking this thing takes energy from me and everyone else, like a vampire. Vampires hate garlic, so I thought maybe…" It sounded stupid when she said it. Like she was grasping at straws and maybe she was.

Julia shrugged and nodded at her. Courtney closed the door. She thought she heard Julia leaving her place in the hallway. Which was weird. Normally they communicated through the cats.

Someone yelled something but it was far enough away

that Courtney didn't catch the words. Something else was happening. Something she didn't quite understand.

She curled up on her bed, deciding to look into vampire legends to see what else might keep them at bay. She needed every advantage. If garlic didn't work, she wanted other ideas.

The moment Mack was cut off from him, Drew felt naked. Vulnerable. He would have rushed to the cat to see if something had happened, but everyone was looking around, acting as if there were a problem.

From the front room, Drew heard Kayley say, "Elmore?" softly, hopefully.

Cari's face paled and she frowned, probably echoing the look he had on his face.

"What happened?" Drew asked.

Cari shook her head. He heard people moving around, mostly upstairs, though Matt's voice yelling for Wilbur came from the basement. Anson ran up the stairs. Elmore, Navy, and Wilbur all stood around in the great room, circling and looking at the humans, puzzled. It didn't take but a moment longer for Mack and Wheelie to appear on the stairs. Both cats jogged over to their people, twining around legs. Drew put a hand on the counter before bending down.

Cari still sat in a chair in the nook. The nook was darker now that Tom had finished putting up the sheets of plywood Drew had brought in. Sweaty, though he wasn't particularly warm, he felt dirty and had no desire to sit on the sofa. He'd shower first.

"Can you hear him?" Cari whispered to Drew.

Kayley came into the main room, Elmore following her. Tears floated in her eyes, though Drew noted the clenched jaw and her clear intention to do what she could to keep them from falling.

Drew shook his head, knowing immediately that Cari had asked if he could hear Mack.

"Me either," Kayley said. Her voice, normally so sure was suddenly soft and girlish. She was the youngest of the clowder, though with her experiences as an EMT and her confidence level, it was easy to forget.

"What happened?" Drew asked, regretting the question almost immediately. If the cats knew, they couldn't share.

Tenny and Tom appeared from upstairs. Tom had changed his shirt after nailing up the boards. He tended to be tidier so it was a surprise to see him in an old red and white baseball shirt. Drew thought maybe he'd been planning to grab the shower Drew himself so badly wanted when the telepathic link had gone silent.

Behind Tenny and Tom came Riley and Stuart. Fin hurried from his room, shaking his head. Amber yawned as she slowly made her way down, staying slightly behind the others, closer to the front room.

"Matt's staying down there with Chase," Anson said quietly. He glared at anyone lest they think Matt wasn't as attached to Wilbur as the rest were to their bond-mates.

"Julia will stay upstairs with Courtney," Cari said. As if the two of them somehow had a telepathic link to each other. "She knows that's important."

Stuart wandered from the great room and into the dim front room. Only a single lamp was lit against the darkness in there. The shutters kept out all the light, but the half-moon shaped window over the front door let in some. Even that was darkening rapidly.

Drew angled himself so that he could watch Stuart, who sank into a chair. He went very still. Probably doing Base Command magic.

Drew smelled something hot, not quite burning, and felt his skin prickle. He absently scratched his arm, noticed that a few others were rubbing the backs of their necks or scratching a leg or an arm. Riley rubbed her hip as if it hurt, but she could have been scratching.

Drew wanted to ask if people thought Stuart was directing his magic at them.

Stuart raised his head when his phone rang. He answered it, giving one and two word answers that told Drew nothing about the conversation.

When the conversation was over, Stuart stood up. "That was Base Command. The cats have reported that all telepathic links are broken. I have a connection to one of the cats at Base Command for the moment. She and I have linked before so it wasn't difficult to re-connect."

It wasn't lost on Drew that Stuart used different terminology than he did for the clowder cats and their bondmates. The link he had to Base Command was clearly a different sort of link.

"What do they think happened?" Kayley asked. "Will we get our telepathic links back?" She looked down at Elmore who was practically sitting on her feet. His brown and black fur appeared slightly raised as if he were cold.

"No one knows," Stuart said. "The clowders in Arizona and Toronto also reported broken telepathic links but the one in Belize is fine, though their link went down for thirteen point two seconds. No one else felt an effect."

If this was the frost witches doing, they had a larger area of effect than Drew had been aware of.

"What about Base Command?" Cari asked. "They're closer than anyone."

"It's winter. None of the queens were ready to breed so there were no bond-mates in Columbus. The links Base Command has with the Command Cats and Cat Home are different, as evidenced by the fact that I can link to Essalyn." Stuart looked at the floor. Trag sat near him but didn't touch him.

Drew crossed his arms over his chest, waiting for Stuart to say more.

"We're more vulnerable. As humans, you give the cats a perspective they don't have otherwise. They have the ability to use your energy via the telepathic link to create magic larger than they can do on their own. Our human abilities are enhanced by our links to the cats, not to mention the fact that they allow us an effective means of communication throughout the house," Stuart said.

"I feel naked," Fin said. He leaned against the wall nearest the main hall. Drew knew what he meant.

From upstairs he heard Julia yell down, "Can I get a shit ton of garlic?"

Drew looked at the others. He frowned, wondering why she wanted garlic. It would be good to know what she knew.

"Courtney has a craving?" Anson asked, shaking his head.

"Garlic works on vampires," Riley said. Drew frowned at her wondering about the non-sequitur.

"I've been reading about what works on monsters that can enchant and do mind control," Riley said. "Vampires came up. They don't like garlic, so I made a note of it. Maybe Courtney thinks that garlic would help her?"

Drew shrugged and ambled over to the kitchen. He didn't feel like doing much of anything, not without Mack to back him up. It was far too quiet in his head without the cat. He looked in the refrigerator and found nothing. Someone else pulled open the bin they held onions and potatoes in and found a couple of bags of garlic.

"I believe she asked for something like a garlic wreath," Stuart said, frowning. A cat must have heard and relayed the information via Stuart's link in Base Command.

"We have one!" Kayley said. "In the basement for decorating in the fall. We have a fake wreath with garlic on it. We can put the real garlic in with it. Maybe she won't notice?"

Tenny hurried into the kitchen and pulled out a pan. "That's a good idea. We can coat the fake garlic with oil and garlic powder and it will stink every bit as much as a real garlic wreath."

"I'll go help you find it," Drew said to Kayley. He wasn't thrilled about going down to the basement where Chase could add more barbs, but what choice did he have?

*A*mber felt adrift. She'd not realized how much Minnett had been grounding her until the telepathic link was severed. The moment the link was gone, Amber had woken up, sitting up in her room, knowing she couldn't go back to sleep. Her world was suddenly internally silent. Outside her door, she'd heard people calling their cats' names and moving around, probably feeling the same sense of wrongness at the sudden loss of their bond-mates.

She'd stumbled out the door and followed the others down to the great room where she'd learned that everyone had lost the link. It wasn't just her. It wasn't even just their clowder but several others.

Stuart talked about the things they lost with the link. For Amber, the magic was far more important. She had basic medical skills, was a decent acupuncturist, but she didn't have the ability to heal the damage done by the frost witches on her own. Even with Minnett's help, she wasn't certain it could be done.

Certainly, Stuart helped by linking with her. When Minnett had been unable to assist in healing, Stuart had offered her energy and guided her the way Minnett might have. But not having the cat at all, not even in the background? Amber wasn't certain she could do anything.

She definitely couldn't help Courtney.

Maybe that was the idea. Of course, the creature or whatever it was, didn't have to block the links to all of them. Amber felt like the link hadn't been severed, not the way Trag had severed his link to Chase. The more she unconsciously reached for the cat, rather like someone pressing a wound, she felt as if there was something blocking her from reaching Minnett.

Julia called for garlic and everyone got busy trying to find it. Like Courtney's need for garlic was all important. Amber thought it was stupid. Of course, without Minnett, garlic might be the best they could do. That and acupuncture.

In the last month, Amber had read more acupuncture theory than she had since school. She'd re-read all her textbooks, ordered others, and taken copious notes on anything that might have a bearing on getting rid of frost witches.

Amber thought of the frost witches as possessing someone. Without Minnett, maybe she ought to go down and get needles. She'd read and made notes on an acupuncture protocol for possession, though whether it included this type of possession, Amber couldn't be certain. Still, she didn't have Minnett to rely on. She had only herself.

Drew went downstairs with Kayley to get garlic, while Tenny began heating butter to melt to create an oil to hold the garlic powder. The smell reached Amber halfway across the kitchen. Tenny wasn't taking any chances about not using enough. She continued through, heading to the medic room in the basement.

Halfway down the stairs, Amber heard Chase talking to Drew. "I told you I was already in the house!"

Chase laughed, but it wasn't a laugh that Amber had ever

heard from him. It sent a shiver up her spine. Mentally, she reached for Minnett, only to hit that wall. She swallowed and continued down the stairs.

She slipped into her medic room to grab needles, closing the door softly. The white cupboards stared silently at her, while the heavily insulated walls protected her from Chase's sarcasm and taunts. This room was for resting. It felt too big and empty without Minnett's voice in her mind. Usually, even when she was alone, cleaning, Minnett was there to keep her company.

Amber placed a box of needles into a plastic container, along with alcohol wipes and a mini-sharps container to hold the used needles. There was nothing to stop Courtney from removing them, but Amber figured even a short insertion time with the correct intent could start the process.

Amber closed her eyes for a few moments to ground herself. She visualized a white light around her. She needed all the psychic protection she could offer herself if she were going to treat Courtney alone. She hadn't mentioned her idea to Stuart. Not only did he have other things on his mind but it was time she stopped asking for his help. It wasn't as if he were a healer.

Opening the door, Amber heard Chase talking

"That's as useless as you are. I'm already here," Chase said. Well, the voice sounded like Chase, though the words didn't. He wasn't normally cruel. Amber knew he was talking to Drew.

Drew said nothing.

Amber stepped out of the room in time to see Chase growing larger. The watcher and guardian cats could do that against a large foe they needed to deal with physically instead of psychically, but Amber had never seen a human do it. Chase stood so tall the hairs on the top of his head brushed the ceiling.

Instinctively, Amber threw a hand out and pushed all her healing energy out, to try and form a barrier around Chase. With Minnett linking to her, she knew she could do it. They surrounded problem areas all the time when working energetically. She hugged the plastic container to her chest with her other arm.

Chase pointed a single finger towards Drew and Kayley, which meant Amber was in the cone.

Sudden cold washed through her. Her teeth chattered. Her skin tightened. She closed her eyes and held her breath against the sudden chill.

If her arm didn't feel frozen she'd have dropped it. But it wouldn't move.

Amber tried to lift her feet. They didn't move.

She tried opening her eyelids, hesitated when she heard the cracking, but needed to know what was going on. She couldn't count on Minnett being there to assist.

She heard Chase laughing.

It made her angry.

That warmed her inside. Amber ran through all the things she was angry about. Having to heal all these people. Having to coddle Drew. Having the fate of worlds on her shoulders. She hadn't signed up for that. Not at all. She was supposed to have help but she was floundering here on her own, making up things as she went, never knowing if she were right or wrong.

All of that fed her anger and she held onto it. She held on to petty irritations like the time someone had laughed at her for saying she was an acupuncturist. She tried to remember all the hateful things she'd heard on social media posts, the ones that made her mad.

Amber went over all the hateful cat jokes. The mean dog jokes.

The heat of her anger kept warming her. Slowly she was able to bring down her arm.

Chase looked over at her. Drew and Kayley were still frozen.

"Get mad," Amber whispered to them, hoping they could still hear.

"Yes. Get mad. I love it when people get mad," Chase said, looking back at her. He picked up a pool cue and wandered back around the table, watching them.

Amber walked up to Drew and Kayley and touched each of them lightly. Their skin was cold, but not frozen. Drew snorted and his face got red. They'd heard her.

Amber took the garlic wreath out of Drew's hand. His fingers flexed enough to let her take it. Matt hurried from his room with a blanket to wrap around them.

It was only then that Amber realized she was cold. She'd been too cold to even notice how chilled she was. She wondered if that was what hypothermia was like.

"If they're really cold, we can use the heat lamp in the medic room," Amber said to Matt. "I should get this upstairs."

Matt nodded.

Drew needed Matt to help him. That would bother him, a lot. The anger in the thought warmed Amber. She smiled.

Then she frowned. She didn't normally take pleasure in someone else's discomfort. It was why Drew's neediness bothered her. She hated being that focus. But there she was, enjoying it.

Reaching the main level Amber went to the kitchen and handed the garlic to Tenny. "I'll let you take this up."

Amber turned to Stuart who was in the corner of the sofa. The cats were around his feet like he was a teacher reading a book to his students.

"I need you to scan my energetic patterns," Amber said. She didn't ask. There wasn't time.

Stuart raised an eyebrow before nodding after a hesitation that was probably brief but was long enough to allow Amber's anger to build again. They needed to hurry. She couldn't save everyone if she were compromised.

"Fin, can you go help Matt with Drew and Kayley?" Stuart asked. Clearly, the cats had told him what happened.

Amber wondered which cat had drawn the short straw and had to monitor Chase and Matt. Probably Wilbur, who would, no doubt, be safely ensconced in Matt's room or peeking out from the hallway.

"Sit," Stuart said as he prepared to scan Amber's energy patterns. She tried to bite back the fear but now that she'd let go of the anger, it was like trying to turn back the tide.

<h1 style="text-align:center">STUART</h1>

Stuart made himself relax. They couldn't lose Amber to the creature. Base Command could require a healer from another clowder to come to Lexington, but it would take time. Last snowfall, the attack had been short and focused. While this one appeared to be hitting harder, perhaps faster, he held out hope it would remain a fairly short attack.

Last time, though, they'd had Amber to try and drive out the frost witches. While Stuart hadn't ever felt that they'd gone away completely, he hoped that they'd hurt them badly enough to drive them into dormancy for a short period.

He rubbed his nose. The smell of garlic made it hard to concentrate. He had no idea how Tenny could stand working on the fake wreath. In the small third-floor bedroom, Courtney might struggle to breathe. Heck, he was down the hall and he might struggle to breathe.

Amber didn't appear to even notice the aroma. Stuart frowned. Had he been infected? The cats left the room, not liking the smell either. He couldn't remember if normal cats were bothered by garlic or not. Not that most normal cats would be stuck in a room that reeked of garlic the way this one did, not unless they lived in a garlic factory.

Apparently, he hated garlic the way many people hated cigarettes.

The low murmur of voices from the kitchen didn't bother him. Even the low murmur of cats in his mind—while he didn't have the telepathic link to Trag that he'd established, he still had his own telepathic abilities—didn't bother him the way the smell did.

Focusing his mind on Amber, Stuart checked over her patterns. She was tired, that was obvious, but nothing else had changed. He opened his eyes.

"I went as deep as I am able without your help, but it appears that you're just depleted. That could be from what happened with Courtney. I don't see anything new," Stuart said. Minnett joined them and put a delicate white paw on Amber's leg.

Amber nodded at the cat.

Stuart watched as Minnett flexed her toes, claws extending slightly, her psychic claws sinking into Amber's thigh, though she wouldn't feel it. Amber looked pale and sad.

Essalyn probably picked up what Stuart was doing and was having Minnett check her over. They needed another healer.

"Riley had a healer cat before Anastasia, didn't she?" Stuart asked aloud, hoping he wouldn't distract Minnett.

"Yes," Tenny said, her voice raised slightly. She picked up the garlic wreath that was now thick and greasy. Extra bulbs of real garlic were tied into the thing. If that didn't keep away Courtney's imaginary vampires, nothing would.

Stuart had been fond of the old-time horror movies, but horror in the movie world was different from the horrors of this one. He missed the dignified evil of Bela Lugosi's

Dracula and the delightful terror of Lon Chaney's monsters. Frankenstein had never really been a horror story for him, though the movies did their best. Chaney may have been the king of makeup in his day but Karloff was probably the best actor among them.

He didn't remember Lugosi's Dracula as being turned off by garlic. Sunshine bothered him. And crosses, though this creature wouldn't subscribe to any human religion to be terrified of such a symbol.

Minnett pulled back her toes. Stuart waited for word from Essalyn.

Her soft voice came soon after. *"Minnett agrees with you. Weakness but no pattern change. She does not appear to have an infection. The attack was more to injure Drew, Kayley, and Amber than to take over."*

The voice was gone as quickly as it had come.

"You're clear," Stuart said.

Amber nodded. "Tired, though. I think you're right about depletion."

Drew and Kayley trudged up the stairs, their feet heavy.

Amber yawned. Stuart did a quick scan, not the thorough one he'd done on Amber—she was far more valuable as the only healer—and saw nothing unusual.

Kayley flopped on the sofa and let her eyes close.

"Food will probably help," Amber said.

"And soda," Kayley said. "Like Mountain Dew maybe. A gallon."

Drew yawned and leaned on the banister.

"Guess I have KP duty," Tenny commented, handing off the wreath to Amber. "Can you take that up? It's as good as I can get it."

It looked pretty good to Stuart, the fresh garlic tied tightly on. The smell about knocked him out and he was glad he didn't have to touch it. He worried his skin would burn.

Amber made a face holding it and kept it away from her body. She grabbed the plastic tub that held her acupuncture paraphernalia.

"Leave them," Stuart said. "You don't have the energy to work on her right now. I want you to sleep some more before you do an acupuncture treatment."

Amber sighed and left her needles. "If someone goes up to the second floor, can you drop them in my room?"

Cari gave her a thumbs up. Tenny had her head in the refrigerator, clearly looking for something to cook up. Drew normally would have taken over, but it was clear he was too tired to be of much help.

"I want to see what that thing does." Stuart moved towards the stairs, leading the way.

Amber nodded, frowning. "She really asked for all that garlic?"

"I believe Julia said a shit ton," Stuart said smiling a little at the image. Did anyone really imagine how much shit that might be? This era had such colorful language and it seemed to get cruder every decade. Of course, every era had its own level of crudeness. The style just changed.

Amber moved slowly up the stairs. Drew followed her, which surprised him a little. Stuart, for all that he still felt fatigued from working on Amber earlier, could have raced them up to the third floor. As it was, he led them from several treads ahead, trying to keep out of choking range of the wreath.

He had no idea if it worked on vampires, but it certainly worked on him.

COURTNEY

Courtney smelled the garlic before anything else. She didn't realize what she was smelling at first, her stomach growling thinking of spaghetti or pizza, hoping that someone was bringing her food. Closer, with the sounds of people walking—several people—she noted the aroma wasn't Italian food, but garlic. Pure garlic.

They'd done it. Courtney hugged the pillow to herself. She was cold but not freezing. Her feet were particularly cold, but then they always tended to be that way. She preferred heavy socks on any day but the hottest afternoons in summertime because otherwise, they'd be cold.

She heard voices talking, softly enough that she couldn't make out the words. Her heart hammered, not in fear but in excitement. The garlic odor was really strong. They'd actually done it. It had to be a garlic wreath.

When the door opened and Amber walked in holding the thing, Courtney couldn't believe it. Amber was holding it out in front of her like she didn't want it too close. Stuart looked pained as if he hated the smell.

Courtney couldn't say she was thrilled with it, but the

scent comforted her. It might keep her internal vampire at bay.

She took the wreath, not liking the greasy feel of it. Noticing that, she realized that many of the garlic bulbs were fake. Someone had coated them in oil and garlic powder. Still, they were sort of papery, which would absorb the odor, keeping it around long after she no longer felt the oil. And there were real bulbs tied around to augment the scent.

The oil would likely get in her hair if she pulled it over her head. Courtney spent a moment debating whether to do so. Her shirt could be ruined, but it wasn't as if she were wearing her favorite clothes. If she went on a killing spree thanks to the darn vampire inside her, it wouldn't matter what she wore anyway.

She pulled it over her head, enjoying the weight of it. That, too, was comforting. That close the garlic odor invaded the very cells of her nose and the back of her throat. No matter what she ate for days it was going to taste like garlic. Not ideal, but a small price if it kept away the witches when she relaxed.

"Are you going to do a healing now?" Courtney asked.

"Do you want me to?" Amber asked.

"No," Stuart said.

Drew hovered behind them, arms crossed. Like he was going to do anything.

Amber glanced at Stuart. Courtney watched him, wondering why he didn't want them to heal her.

"I do," Courtney said. She frowned wondering Julia had told them she was ready to die and Stuart had decided to kill her. "Are you going to kill me instead?"

Amber looked horrified. If there had been a discussion, she clearly hadn't thought about the idea of killing Courtney. That might be good.

Drew was impassive. Almost hopeful or maybe he was relieved that someone else brought it up.

Stuart started shaking his head immediately, backing up a step, distancing himself from her questions. Or maybe the garlic. He was holding a hand over his nose. If she could take wearing the thing, he ought to be able to stand being in the same room with it.

"I think Amber was depleted when the entity attacked her last time she tried examining you. Just a little while ago, she was downstairs and Chase attacked her, Drew, and Kayley."

Courtney noted how watchful Stuart was. No doubt he wanted to see how she reacted, probably wondering if she'd known or somehow been involved. Courtney hadn't known anything about the attack. Hadn't felt anything. She hadn't even been sleeping. She'd been playing a game on her phone, not really relaxing but not really paying attention. It was enough to keep her awake without forcing her to confront the fact that she'd voluntarily imprisoned herself in the attic room.

The garlic perked her up almost like coffee perked her up in the morning.

"What did he do?" Courtney asked, wondering if they'd tell her.

"He used some sort of cold blast against us," Amber said. Her eyes were narrow like she was looking for tells.

It made Courtney angry that they all seemed ready to believe that she'd know about what Chase had done. She rubbed her hand against the greasy wreath. She'd not been sent to the field of dying flowers. She'd been awake.

"You're okay?" Courtney asked. She hoped she didn't sound disappointed.

Amber nodded.

Drew glared at her.

Stuart was watchful. "May I examine your energetic patterns?"

He was very polite about it. At least this time, they were asking her and not just doing things to her in a room in the basement.

Courtney nodded, backing up to sit on the daybed. She didn't lean back, didn't want the grease on the blankets. Of course, later on, it would get on them when she tried to sleep. Maybe the grease would have seeped into the wreath by then. Later, she would shower off the icky feeling and change clothes, ready for bed. She didn't have a television in there but she had her laptop and a phone to keep her occupied.

Stuart followed, though his nose wrinkled and his hand stayed covering his face.

He didn't kneel but half-closed his eyes like a dog getting a particularly good belly rub and looked towards her. Courtney didn't know what to do while he worked. She felt weird. Amber was watching Stuart. Drew, however, was staring at her as if he could see things, too.

Stuart backed up quickly, his eyes fully open. "It's still mostly dark but it isn't as dark, I don't think. In a few hours after Amber rests, we can try a treatment."

Courtney nodded. "I'll be here." Like she was going to go anywhere.

No one said good-bye, really, just leaving her with the wreath. Courtney looked out the window, but darkness had fallen. Lights from the house across the street glowed in the darkness which allowed her to see that the snowfall hadn't abated. Angling herself around to see the driveway meant pressing her nose against the cold glass, smearing it with the garlic oil from the wreath around her neck. Courtney noted that her car was half-buried in the white stuff.

It hadn't let up in the least bit. Before, it had snowed on and off. This was coming down hard and steady.

She grabbed her phone and started looking at the weather. The temperature had dropped to below zero numbers. She didn't think that had happened in Lexington in her lifetime, not that she was a weather watcher. That kind of chill would have made the news, though.

The snow was expected to continue through at least the next day. Meteorologists were puzzled by where the moisture was coming from.

Courtney could have told them. It was the thing inside her. People wouldn't believe her. They'd think she was crazy, lock her up in some sanitarium. Maybe that was another option. She could talk about what was going on and normal people would lock her up somewhere, drug her up so that she couldn't hurt anyone if she tried. Unfortunately, if drugs only worked on her and not the entity, she'd lose the fight before it began.

No. The clowder house had been the right move.

Chase was using cold blasts. Like he could control it. Courtney closed her eyes and wondered what it would be like to have that sort of power.

The garlic kept her from focusing on her fantasy. It wouldn't hurt to take the wreath off for just a few minutes so she could relax. Maybe she could lie down without having to worry about getting the covers greasy.

Before she knew it, Courtney was walking into the bathroom to lay the wreath down on the sink counter. She didn't want the smell so close. She closed the door.

The stink permeated her clothing and her nose, impossible to ignore. Courtney wanted to scream in anger.

The angry heat warmed her. She shook her head, her hands going to her neck, realizing suddenly that she'd taken the wreath off. Except she hadn't meant to do that, not really.

Courtney leaned forward and put her hands over her face. The oil in the garlic had left a lingering aroma on her fingers and she pulled them away. After feeling hopeless for not being able to keep the wreath on, being able to be controlled to take it off, Courtney suddenly smiled.

If garlic didn't work, the vampire inside her wouldn't have made her take the wreath off. Courtney went back to the bathroom to put it back around her neck.

AMBER

Amber couldn't see the clock when she woke. She was just suddenly jarred awake, wide awake, not groggy from a deep sleep, though it took her a moment to orient herself. She searched, automatically, for Minnett, who would tell her the time, but no one was there. They'd been cut off. The day came back to Amber.

Sitting up, Amber saw the dark outline of the tuxedo cat on the foot of the bed, curled up, her nose pressed to her back feet, tail slightly covering it. As Amber moved and the blankets pulled at her, Minnett looked up, her large golden eyes glowing faintly in the dark. Outside the room, the hall light was on.

Most nights it was turned off, but Amber wasn't surprised that it was on that night. Someone was up, keeping watch. She looked closely at the clock, her slightly blurred vision clearing as her mind began to make sense of the pre-dawn world around her.

She'd slept deeply and hard without a single dream, something that surprised her given everything going on. Courtney had talked about weird dreams the last time she'd been in the house. Amber had half expected to find herself wandering about in a strange landscape, perhaps a childhood home, locked in her room, unable to come out.

That hadn't ever happened to her, of course. She'd never been locked in her room, though her parents had both been neglectful, bordering on abusive. Amber had fended for herself for most of her childhood. Both her parents were attorneys, working long hours, making money, being available for clients. They were successful, and Amber had had a series of nannies until she had grown up—if you could consider twelve years old grown-up.

By the time the last nanny had been fired for something Amber couldn't remember, probably having a boyfriend over when her parents hadn't gotten home at the agreed-upon time, it had been decided Amber could take care of herself for the short time between the end of school and when one of her parents got home. They'd been good for about two weeks after that, at least one of them home on time. Sometimes Amber thought it was just long enough to learn that she could cook for herself and not burn the house down.

If anything, being locked in her room would have been a luxury because someone else would have been taking care of her.

Amber threw on a KU sweatshirt and fleece-lined black leggings, heavy socks, and big slippers that looked like tuxedo cats, and headed out of the room. She heard voices downstairs, strained her ears to hear who it might be but couldn't make them out.

Shadows reached for her from the library. The darker shadow of a cat watching out the window turned to stare at her. Probably Trag. He'd have no one to cuddle against, worried about the severing of the mind-bonds. Although, was it really severing if Amber felt the bond there, the link, but just couldn't get to Minnett?

Minnett hurried down the stairs in front of her, her white feet bouncing in anticipation of an early breakfast. She often acted like a real cat, a plain, ordinary kitty cat. If not for the bond, it would be easy for Amber to think of her that way.

Once in the great room, walking towards the kitchen, Amber noted that Fin was there with Tenny.

"You're up early," Tenny said.

"Are you up late or early?" Amber asked.

"A little of both. I napped after cooking for everyone and then got up for night watch." Tenny rested her arms on the table.

Fin sipped from his coffee, which he held in both hands. "I'm here to relieve her for the early shift." The bright lights should have made the room look cheerful but with the boards up and the gray shadows from the shuttered front room, it felt gloomy.

Amber started making tea. She normally drank coffee but she was so awake that morning that she wanted tea. "Who's downstairs?"

After feeding Minnett, Amber found some toaster pastries. Not too much for that early but enough to perk her up.

"Anson took the night shift. Matt is sleeping. He'll have Chase and the day shift, probably playing pool again," Fin said.

Amber nodded. "I'll finish my tea and go check on Courtney. I want to try an acupuncture treatment. If it does anything for her, maybe it will work on Chase."

Fin frowned.

"What?"

"He hates needles," Fin said. "He's going to do everything he can to avoid it. If what I'm hearing from yesterday is any indication, it's quite a bit. We really need our bond-mates back."

Fin was right. That wasn't something Amber knew how to fix. She hoped they weren't expecting that of her, particularly when she didn't even have all of her power.

"I wonder if they sent someone from outside the affected area to one of the affected clowders, would they also lose the link to their bond-mate," Amber said. She thought about it, hoping to remember to tell Stuart to suggest it to Base Command. The human could go. The cat would stay. See what happened. The human could return.

"Are you thinking of having them send another healer?" Tenny asked. Amber needed to remember that Tenny always knew far more than she let on. She stayed quiet a lot of the time, listening. She absorbed everything.

"If they have to," Amber said. "I wish they would."

"What about Riley?" Fin asked.

"What about her?" Amber wasn't sure where he was going with the question.

"Her first bond-mate was a healer cat. Louisa, I think." Fin sipped some more coffee. He was looking more awake.

Amber bit into her pastry. She'd chosen blueberry that morning. The frosting dripped off it, too thickly applied and too watery to stay on. She pushed the dollop onto her finger and licked it off. Sugar was energy. She needed all the energy she could get. Quickly. And easily.

"You think she can help?" Amber hadn't really thought about Riley. She seemed happy enough to be up in her library researching things and making notes on the creatures the clowder dealt with, having Anastasia send that information to Base Command. Riley didn't talk about healing but she'd started out life as a nurse and then been brought into the clowder when she was about Amber's age. She'd just never left.

If asked, Riley tended to deflect saying it had been ages and medicine had changed so much that she'd not be any help. Amber wondered what Riley's healing power had looked like. And why she never seemed inclined to use it even on herself. Riley often came to Amber for some relief of her hip pain and stiffness but the problem was progressing. It was worse with the snow, though Amber didn't know if that was a natural progression of the arthritis, or if it was the cold, or some unique aspect of the frost witch incursion.

The three of them went quiet. Fin drank his coffee. Amber ate her pastry. Tenny leaned back, apparently relaxed, but the slight tension in her shoulders said she was alert for anything happening.

Voices drifted up from downstairs. It sounded like Chase was awake.

"Anyone want to play pool?" Chase called from the basement, his voice reaching them.

Fin shook his head and rolled his eyes.

"That'd be a no," Tenny called back. "Some of us have to work." Looking at Amber and Fin, she lowered her voice. "And some of us have to sleep."

Amber smiled at her and ate another bite of pastry, enjoying the spurt of berry flavor in her mouth. She could get addicted to those things and that was probably a bad thing.

Chase didn't respond.

Amber felt something pulling at her, a small tug at her feet. The cats weren't around, but her feet were being tugged at. She frowned, moving them. Nothing was there.

"Do you feel that?" Amber asked.

"What?" Fin asked.

"Your feet?" She didn't want to say too much, give them ideas. She needed to know what they, themselves felt.

Tenny stared straight ahead, thinking. "Something is tugging at them. Feels like a fish on a line."

"Do you think it's Chase?" Amber asked. He'd just gotten up, started playing pool. If they were really playing down there, she wondered how he was able to grab energy while doing so.

"Or Courtney, but I'd expect her to tug at my head," Fin said quietly. He got up and moved from the table.

Amber followed. The tug went with her, disappearing when she left the great room. Unfortunately, once she returned and sank onto the sofa, it began again.

She moved to the front room. Sitting there, finishing her tea, the tugging didn't start again. For the moment, Chase only had access to the great room. Kayley and Tom had rooms above it.

"This could make day watch interesting," Fin said, following Amber into the front room. Tenny was right behind him.

"No one's caught my little toes now," she giggled. "It's got to be him. Sapping us."

"He's being more open about it," Amber said.

"He's confident," Tenny said. "I'm not sure about Courtney. She seems to want to get rid of this thing. Chase doesn't even seem to be fighting. Not anymore."

"Maybe it was stronger in him," Amber suggested. Her impression of Courtney was a whiny, needy woman. Amber hadn't understood what Chase had seen in her. Maybe she was wrong. Maybe Courtney possessed a core of strength that Amber hadn't noticed. She didn't want to get her hopes up.

After finishing her tea, Amber went into the kitchen to wash her cup out. She made note of how her feet felt as she walked across the floor. No tugs as long as she was moving but in the short time it took her to wash out the mug and put in the drying rack, she felt something. Her toes were colder than normal, too.

Something to tell Stuart later. "I'm going to go up and see about giving Courtney a treatment."

"It's not even six in the morning," Tenny said. She had her feet up on the sofa, like that might protect them. Amber doubted it, but she understood the impulse. Tenny, at least, was limber enough to flow into a fighting stance in an instant.

"Beggars can't be choosers," Amber said lightly. "Maybe this will surprise her or the entity. Besides, I don't know what sorts of things Stuart will expect me to do when he wakes up."

Fin smiled. Tenny said nothing, turning her head to listen outside. "I think I hear something."

She was up, standing near the front door, Fin beside her, both ready for battle when someone started ringing the doorbell and banging on the hurricane shutters.

Tenny looked at Fin and rolled her eyes.

"I guess she'll be awake for that treatment," Amber said, hurrying up to the second floor to get her needles. Minnett had left the main room even before Amber had felt Chase pulling energy. She wondered if the cats felt it and that's why they'd been less inclined to use the great room. Or maybe they felt something but couldn't place what it was.

She passed Tom on his way down, still buttoning a flannel shirt. Kayley was right behind him, though she still wore pajama bottoms. She'd put on a shirt and her shoes and that was it.

Riley's door opened and she looked out.

Amber shook her head. Riley didn't close the door but she moved back into the shadows of her room.

Hurrying down the hallway, the banging was loud enough and hard enough that Amber felt it through her body. Hopefully, the people out there would go away before too long. She didn't think she could stand hours of that. None of them could.

Amber didn't see Minnett when she got to her room to grab the plastic container she'd put together yesterday. Perhaps the cats would get together and do what they could with their magic to keep the people at bay.

She wondered if they'd be powerful enough without their telepathic link to their humans.

DREW

*D*rew was practically dressed before he was fully awake. The pounding on the windows, the boards, and the shutters, even the front door from the sound of it, echoed around him. The metal shutters thrummed and hummed with echoing clanks. He didn't hear glass shattering, but it must have happened as he heard the deep hammering of tools against wood.

Hopefully, the plywood could hold out.

Shoes last. Mack had already left the room, hurrying to the door the moment Drew sat up. He only remembered the cat had been there in hindsight. He missed the ability to know exactly where Mack was, whether in the great room or upstairs in the library or somewhere else in the house.

Drew didn't believe Mack would have gone to the basement. The cats had been avoiding getting too near Chase since the first snowfall, though they would sometimes go to the medic room or perhaps Matt or Anson's rooms.

Tenny and Fin were in the front room, both of them ready for fighting. Tenny waited closer to the front door. Fin was over closer to the shutters in the living room, though Drew didn't think anyone would come through there.

Anson waited by the boarded-up windows in the great room. Tom waited with him. Footsteps hurried down the stairs. Cari and Julia.

Drew looked around for a weapon. He went to the closet and got a broom. The handle would allow him to push people back. He stood with it, ready against anyone breaching the back windows.

"What about the basement?" Drew asked.

Tom glanced at him, noted the people around the room, and nodded. He went downstairs. Julia followed. Only then did Drew noticed she carried a taser.

Cari had pepper spray.

The banging went on but the wood held. No one came with an ax for which Drew was glad.

Stuart didn't appear but at some point, the banging stopped. He heard some screams and cries from outside. Drew wanted to know what was happening. Mack would have told him. The cats, at least some of them, would be watching from upstairs. They'd see what was going on.

Drew sighed as things quieted. His feet itched. Something was tickling them as he stood in the room. He frowned.

"We think it's Chase," Tenny said coming back to the great room. Her face looked drawn. She'd been up all night, watching.

"We ought to knock him out," Drew said. "Do we have a tranquilizer or something? Or can the cats knock him out?"

"We can ask Stuart when he comes down," Fin said. He was still in the entry, keeping an eye on the door. After speaking, he got the step stool from the closet tucked into the corner between the stairs and front door. He stepped up on it and peered through the upper windows.

"They're standing back. Several are rubbing their arms,"

Fin said. "Quite a group of them. Sticks and knives, but no one thought to bring an ax that I can see, although there's a sledgehammer."

Drew waited with the others, wondering how soon the people would come back. He heard someone moving upstairs, hoped it was Stuart so he could tell them what was going on, but whoever it was took the stairs up and not down. Stuart was on the third floor so it had to be Riley or Amber, perhaps checking on Courtney.

Stuart didn't appear. Drew got antsy.

He looked at the others, all frowning, wondering what was going on.

"I'll go check on him," Drew said quietly. He knew everyone realized he was talking about Stuart.

He walked past the basement stairs. He thought he heard Chase laughing but it might have been his imagination.

It felt good to be out of the great room. His body felt stronger. Drew wondered if anyone else noticed the changes. He didn't have time to ask. If it wasn't just his imagination, then others would notice the sensation, too.

He didn't see anyone on the second floor. If Riley was around, she was tucked in her room or back in the library. Drew hurried up to the third floor. Kayley was outside Courtney's room, looking towards the open door. Drew considered going down to talk to her, but she said something to someone inside. Kayley wasn't in danger. Not then.

Drew went to the left and knocked on the door that belonged to Stuart. The room itself was a decent size, with a decent bathroom but there was little furniture. As things had gotten old and worn, furniture had been taken from that room to be used elsewhere. All that was left was an old mattress, probably one someone intended to give away at some point, and a dresser.

The empty room just down the hall was actually

furnished, but Stuart had chosen this one. Drew didn't understand why.

He heard no one moving around inside. He twisted the knob. It wasn't locked, thankfully. He poked his head into the darkened room. Faint light came through the broken slats of the blinds—something else that ought to be fixed—so that Drew made out a figure lying back on the mattress. He stepped inside, staring at Stuart.

The man's chest rose and fell in shallow, slow breaths. His arms had fallen to the sides of his body. His lips remained pressed together.

Stuart touched a leg, lightly just to see what would happen. Stuart didn't move.

Drew shook the leg a little, hoping that would be enough and Stuart would open his eyes.

Nothing twitched or moved. Drew knew that even if Stuart were deep in a trance to do the magic protecting the clowder house that he would have moved, or opened his eyes upon being shaken.

Drew took a step towards the head of the bed. He shook Stuart's shoulder, hard. Stuart's head lolled from side to side as if he were dead.

His chest continued to rise and fall. He wasn't dead, but something was wrong.

Drew slipped out of the room to talk to Amber. He glanced back at Kayley and saw that Amber was just coming out of Courtney's room. Good. He needed her.

COURTNEY

*C*ourtney woke to the sounds of pounding. The garlic wreath hung around her neck, making her hair and body feel greasy and gross. Even the sheets were slimy from oil. She'd habituated to the smell, mostly. It made her cough a little more. Dinner had been a plain chicken sandwich which had tasted as if she'd doused it in garlic sauce.

Going to the bathroom, she noted that her skin was red and irritated where the garlic oil had touched it directly. The areas beneath the t-shirt that she slept in appeared to be fine. The heavier shirt she'd been wearing the day before hung in the shower, drying. It had felt too greasy to continue wearing so Courtney had washed it out in there.

Amber knocked on the door as Courtney had made her way back to the bed, wondering whether she'd get any sleep. It was far too early.

"I figured you'd be awake with all the pounding," Amber said.

Courtney nodded. She remembered being in the medic room in the basement last time. There, the pounding had only been background noise. She didn't feel the rhythmic movement of the house down there, nor did the sounds seem to echo in her bones, making her teeth feel as if they were rattling.

"I didn't do it," Courtney said. "At least I don't think so. I wasn't in the field of dying flowers. I'm usually there when something happens."

Amber ignored her comment. Instead, she held up a plastic container.

"I'd like to do an acupuncture treatment," Amber said.

"I guess," Courtney said. She'd not had acupuncture before and wasn't sure what it entailed. "What do I need to do?"

"I'm going to insert some needles in particular places on your body. I'll need to get to your abdomen, your upper thigh, and your ankle. It might best if you took off your pajama bottoms and then lifted your top. You can put a blanket partly over you. I'll go out and let you change," Amber said.

"Okay." It appeared Courtney wasn't going to be given a choice. She didn't like having to strip down but she made herself as comfortable as possible. When she was done, she called out that she was ready.

Her voice sounded extra loud because the moment she yelled, the pounding stopped. Just stopped, all of a sudden as if everyone or everything outside pounding was gone. As Amber walked back in and started taking things out of her container, Courtney wondered if the sudden silence was a good thing or not.

Amber showed her the first needle. It was a tiny silver thing that didn't appear much wider than a hair. Amber had taken it out of a little tube, which she called a guide tube. She threw away that needle after moving it a bit to show Courtney how small and flexible it was.

Courtney laid back, waiting. The first needle was inserted

in the middle of her belly, towards her breasts. It didn't feel like much when it went in. The next needle was placed on the right side of her belly button just at the edge of her little belly pouch. Again, that one didn't hurt.

Amber moved the blanket to insert the one in her thigh. It was so high and towards the middle that Courtney felt uncomfortable with the placement but Amber did nothing more than insert the needle and move on before adjusting the blanket around it. Then she placed one in Courtney's ankle.

Finishing that Amber moved backward going up her left side. With the last needle inserted, everything began to ache. The garlic bothered Courtney more, making her cough.

"Everything okay?" Amber asked.

"The garlic smells stronger," Courtney said. Her eyes were watering. For once they weren't watering because she was upset but because the stink of garlic was over-powering.

Amber watched for a few minutes. Nothing happened. Courtney didn't go into respiratory arrest.

"How long?" Courtney asked, wondering when Amber would start taking out the needles.

"It depends on you," Amber said. "I'm getting a sense for how the needles are placed in your body. It's kind of how they look, which is weird, I know. I'll be coming in now and then, looking for any changes."

Courtney had thought the needles would only be in for a few minutes. Her skin started to feel itchy around the points.

"You'll want to lay back and try and relax as much as possible," Amber said.

Courtney nodded, trying to still her hands. Amber opened the door and talked to Kayley. Then she said something to someone with a lower voice, probably a man. Courtney couldn't hear what they were saying. She strained to listen but Amber shut the door, leaving Courtney alone with the needles.

She could easily pull them out. No one would know. Her fingers twitched, aching to do so, but Courtney laid there. The itchiness turned into an ache. Now she felt the needles. The one in the middle of her upper abdomen started to throb as if it were just now being pushed in, the ache radiating out around her sides and then down towards her back.

Courtney closed her eyes against the pain. Her eyes had been barely closed for a moment and she was in the field of dying flowers. There had been no smells there, not the faintest odor of rot. However, this time she still smelled the garlic.

Looking down at where her feet should be, she saw the garlic wreath. Courtney tried to make sense of the place. She'd been wearing the wreath. Here, she seemed to have no body but the wreath had come with her and was lying on the ground.

Peering closer at it, she noted fumes coming off of it. The flowers nearest seemed redder than they had been before. Courtney thought they might stand a bit taller, too.

She heard someone tramping through her field. She turned, or thought she turned—it was hard to say given that she had no real body.

Stuart stood just off to the side of her, looking down at the wreath.

"Stuart?" Courtney said.

He looked up. A furrow grew between his eyes. "Court-ney?" The inflection of the word went up at the end. A question. He looked around.

"You can't see me?" Courtney asked. Of course, why should he? She couldn't see herself.

"No."

"I'm right next to you," Courtney said. "That's my wreath."

"But you still ended up here," Stuart said.

"With the wreath."

"Did you come here before or after the pounding started?" Stuart asked. Even here, Courtney noted that he appeared to be trying to figure out the mystery. Perhaps she had underestimated him thinking he was just weird. Maybe he was one of those odd geniuses that didn't understand social norms.

"After. Amber came in and gave me an acupuncture treatment," Courtney said. "Everything hurt. I closed my eyes to try and ignore the pain until she came back. I didn't even fall asleep. I was just here."

"I've been wandering in the field for a few minutes," Stuart said. "I put up a barrier around the house. Essalyn helped me link to the cats so it was powerful. Then I lay back to recover my energy and I ended up here. I wonder why you can see me but I can't see you?"

Courtney didn't understand half of what he said. She had no idea who Essalyn was or why he was recovering energy. It sounded all woo woo. A part of her, even there, in that weird situation wanted to ignore his ramblings as those of a crazy man.

She'd already gone so far down the crazy road of alternate realities and things that didn't belong in her normal, practical world that she told herself she could be okay with a man who could raise a barrier and recoup his energies.

"I don't know," Courtney said. "Maybe because I was here first?"

"Maybe…" Stuart sounded thoughtful as if she might be more right than she thought.

Courtney waited, noticing that the flowers around the garlic wreath were definitely brighter red. Perhaps the garlic was healing them.

"Can you smell the garlic?" Courtney asked.

Stuart shook his head. "How did you get out of here?"

"I just focused on my body and I was back there all of a sudden," Courtney said.

Stuart closed his eyes, probably trying to imagine his body. Nothing happened. Courtney didn't understand why it was different for him.

"Maybe pick up the garlic wreath," Courtney said. It helped the flowers.

Stuart did. Closed his eyes again. Nothing happened.

Courtney reached out to touch him. She felt nothing at first but focused on her hand touching Stuart's hand. She couldn't see her hand but she felt it getting cold.

She pulled the coldness with her, imagining that she was bringing Stuart with her out of the field of dying flowers.

In the next moment, Courtney felt her body. It was heavy and achy. Her stomach felt vaguely nauseous. Her ears rang. She felt cold, especially her right hand, which was the one she'd imagined bringing Stuart out of the field with.

"Amber?" Courtney called. No one came.

She moved to sit up, but the needles in her belly ached even more deeply. The pain radiated down her belly and into her legs. Courtney laid back, hoping the ache would go away. It stayed and continued to get worse.

Amber said she'd be there to help.

"Hey!" Courtney called again, louder. "These hurt!"

Kayley poked her head in the door. "It will be a few until Amber can get here, okay? Just keep breathing. I don't think she wants to take the needles out just yet."

"Okay," Courtney said in a small voice. Her eyes began to water again. This time it wasn't the garlic, which, she realized, she'd hardly noticed since getting back from the field of dying flowers, but because she hurt and she was scared.

Hearing about Courtney's field of dying flowers had given Stuart a particular image. He'd imagined red roses falling from their bushes, the petals covering the ground like blood splatter.

What he found when he was there was completely different. The flowers looked more like red poppies falling over. If it had come from his mind, Stuart would have thought it was a testament to those fallen in a war long over. Courtney was too young to be thinking of World War I.

The fact that she could see him but he couldn't see her was interesting. The garlic wreath coming with her into the field also perplexed him.

He'd felt a tug and suddenly he was back in his body. He smelled garlic, faintly. Along with that was a clean laundry scent he associated with Amber.

"Stuart?" Amber asked, shaking him slightly.

He opened his eyes.

"Thank god! I couldn't wake you!" Amber said.

"I got pulled into Courtney's field of dying flowers,"

Stuart said, sitting up. He moved more slowly than was his normal want, making sure he had no dizziness.

"How?" Amber asked.

Stuart took a moment to think about what had happened. Drew stood by the door, arms crossed, waiting for him to suggest he was part of the problem.

"I don't know," Stuart said. "Essalyn helped me link to the cats and we created a shield that would repel everyone banging on the shutters and boards. I finished that and laid back to rest, examining my own energy levels. I felt more drained than I should have. Then I was in the field."

"Could Courtney have brought you?" Drew asked. He glanced over his shoulder towards the hall.

"Courtney brought me out," Stuart said. "I ran into her there. She had the wreath with her. She told me how she got out but it didn't work for me. Instead, she pulled at my arm and I landed here, on my mattress."

"I'm giving her a treatment," Amber said. "She shouldn't have gone to the field."

Stuart pushed himself up. "Let's go check on her."

Drew let them pass, intending to follow rather than lead. He glared at Stuart when Stuart passed him. It was all Stuart could do not to sigh. Drew was beginning to annoy him.

Kayley stood outside the door, leaning against the wall. "She was asking for you." No doubt meaning Courtney.

"You know why?" Amber asked before opening the door.

"I think the needles were hurting," Kayley said.

Stuart waited while Amber went in first. He noted that Courtney was wearing her garlic wreath. The smell reached him even at the door, stronger than it was in the field. It brought up the bile in the back of his throat. He didn't know if he'd ever eat spaghetti again. He used to like garlic but this… this stink overwhelmed everything.

"You made it!" Courtney said, looking past Amber at Stuart.

"I did," he said.

Courtney smiled and nodded. Her top teeth pulled at her bottom lip. He got the impression of shy pride, as if she felt she'd done something worthwhile, something she'd never expected. Reflecting for a moment, Stuart realized she was right. No one would have expected her to succeed where others failed.

"How are the needles?" Amber asked. She didn't quite brush away Courtney's pride but almost.

"They hurt. And my stomach feels gross," Courtney said.

"Describe gross," Amber said.

"At first it was like I was going to puke, but now it's more like my whole stomach wants to crawl up my throat and leave. And everything hurts. I mean the needles ache right there but the ache goes everywhere. Really deep, like into my back from this one in the front."

Stuart watched Amber examine the needles. He didn't know what she was looking for. He unfocused his eyes and looked at Courtney's energetic patterns. They hadn't changed exactly but they were stronger, brighter. Like Courtney had come more alive. He hoped that was a good thing. Later, he'd need Amber to lead him through Courtney's energy fields so he could get a closer look at what was going on.

"Can you think about re-linking the bond-mates," Stuart asked.

"What?" Drew snapped. "She can't!"

"What do you mean?" Courtney asked.

Amber turned to stare at him, her eyes large.

"The bond-mates can't hear their cats. Their telepathic link has been interfered with. Can you fix that?" Stuart asked.

"I don't know," Courtney said.

"Try," Stuart ordered.

Drew glared at him even harder.

Fortunately, everyone was mad at him and not at Courtney. Stuart doubted if they'd turned their ire on her that she'd have succeeded in fixing the bond. He waited while she closed her eyes.

Stuart lowered his eyelids a little, once again examining her energy. It was still brighter. The needles shone golden in that realm and appeared to be feeding her energy. Dark swirls were being pulled out, or maybe mixed in with more golden light, reducing the shadow but not removing it. He looked forward to examining Courtney's energy further.

He tried reaching out to Trag. The blockage felt narrower. He could almost hear the cat, closer than usual.

"Here…" was all Stuart heard.

"There." The voice was Trag's. Stuart had only heard it once, so very briefly, but he recognized it.

He waited, listening, but no other words came through. He heard mumbles but couldn't quite make them out. He was so close.

Courtney opened her eyes. "I don't even know what re-linking would look like. I thought about plugging in a computer to the internet, you know, and picturing it linking up. Did that work?"

"No," Amber said.

"If you end up in the field of dying flowers, think about talking to cats and letting cats talk to their people. Maybe something will come to you there," Stuart said. He didn't mention that he thought she'd done something, at least a little something. The others didn't hear as well as he did. Maybe they hadn't heard their bond-mates at all.

"Likely," Essalyn's voice echoed in his mind. "The cats heard their people for a moment but they couldn't really get through. I suggest you find Trag in the library and try talking to him in close proximity. You heard something from him and he can still pick up on about half of your thoughts, which is more than the other cats can do with their bond-mates."

Stuart turned to leave the room.

"Where are you going?" Drew demanded.

"To the library," Stuart said. "There's nothing more for me to do here while Amber works with Courtney."

Drew hesitated, lifting one foot and then the other. Stuart enjoyed the fact that Drew wasn't sure who to stay with. Protect Amber from Courtney who wasn't much of a threat right at the moment, or follow Stuart, who may or may not be a threat in Drew's mind.

Stuart really didn't care what Drew decided. He wanted to see if he could communicate with Trag when they were closer together.

AMBER

It felt wrong to tell Courtney about the blocked link to the telepathic cats. Stuart was being reckless. Nothing Amber could do about it though.

She rested her fingers on Courtney's wrist, feeling her pulses on that side. Ideally, Amber would be feeling pulses on both sides, but the daybed pressed up against the wall made things awkward.

Having never done a five element possession treatment before—Amber's training was not in that particular theory of Chinese Medicine—she wasn't sure what she was looking for. According to what she'd read, Courtney should appear more present in the room. Courtney had appeared present in most cases, except when she was unconscious. Maybe this treatment needed to be done if Courtney fell unconscious again, to the entity.

"It hurts," Courtney said.

"Where?" Amber asked.

"All over. It's like all the aches are joined together in one big line. I feel like my body is turning inside out," Courtney said.

"I want to leave the needles," Amber said, trying to sound confident, like she knew what she was talking about. Even if she had used the treatment before, she'd never used it on someone possessed by something outside the world. The cats understood symbionts and how to remove those if they became a problem, but this wasn't a symbiotic entity. This was something that wanted to possess Courtney. Amber had a feeling it needed Courtney to take over the world—though, perhaps eat the world would be more accurate.

"Okay." Courtney's voice sounded like a little girl, agreeing to something she hated, about to cry. Amber left her there and went out to the hallway. She closed the door softly. Kayley sat on the floor, playing on her phone. Someone had brought up a blanket.

Amber felt something in the back of her mind, almost the way she would feel Minnett but she heard nothing from the cat. It was disorienting. For a moment she worried she'd been infected, but Stuart had examined her and so had Minnett.

Amber looked back at the door. She thought of Courtney lying there, the fact that the needles hurt so much. They wouldn't bother most people. Most people would go to sleep. Something was happening. She wanted to see what it was, perhaps guide it. Minnett would help her if they were connected.

"You have EMT training, right?" Amber asked Kayley.

Kayley nodded.

"I'm going to need some backup. I'll get Riley to help, too."

Kayley looked puzzled but she didn't say much. Amber felt her watching her as she hurried to the stairs.

She found Stuart in the library with Trag. She didn't want to run into him. Across the hall, Riley's doorway was still partly open. Gray daylight had come while they'd been talking to Courtney.

Amber knocked on Riley's door. As she'd hoped, Riley came out of the bathroom. She was fully dressed in jeans and a green sweatshirt with a little cream collar around the top. The sweatshirt had a picture of a cat and Christmas tree on it, surrounded by a wreath of snow. Riley had another sweatshirt like it with a snowman on it. This was probably the more appropriate shirt, all things considered.

"What's up?" Riley asked.

"I don't have Minnett and I need back up with Courtney. I thought since you had a healer bond-mate once, that you'd understand more than other people. I'm also having Kayley work with me," Amber said. She kept her voice low. She didn't want Stuart to hear, or perhaps, even worse, Drew. He'd offer energy if needed but didn't know how to protect himself. Amber wasn't at all certain how to convey to him ways to protect himself if he were offering energy, either. It wasn't something she did, not like that.

"Okay," Riley said. She didn't seem thrilled with the idea but she didn't say no. As Amber walked back up the stairs, Riley followed, close enough that Amber smelled the mint scent of toothpaste she must have just used. The stairwell creaked and groaned, probably echoing the pains in Riley's hips.

Once outside Courtney's door, with Kayley standing, waiting, Amber told them what she needed.

"I'm going to have Riley support me. If she can, I want her to hold onto me and look over my shoulder as I look at Courtney's energy field. I'll have you a little further back. Intervene if something appears to go wrong," Amber said.

"I've never done an energy scan, not without Louisa," Riley said. Her voice hitched slightly. Being blocked from

Anastasia was no doubt reminding her of the pain of losing her first bond-mate.

"Let's see if I can take Louisa's place, then," Amber said. She didn't know if she could but it was worth a try. She wanted eyes on her. "If you don't see anything, just keep focusing on me. If anything makes you think something has gone wrong, pull me out."

Riley nodded. She was still nervous, more nervous than Amber would have liked, but Riley was really all she had. Kayley might have more recent medical skills but she'd never worked as a bond-mate healer.

The three of them went into the room. Courtney opened her eyes when the door opened. Her head turned slightly towards them. Her lips turned down, more a frown of puzzlement about all three of them than a dislike.

"I'm going to check your energy if that's okay," Amber said.

"Sure. Whatever." Courtney raised her shoulders in a half shrug. She bit back a small moan, though it was audible enough to Amber. The needles were really hurting her.

Amber knelt by the bed. Riley looked around for a chair, but there wasn't one. She slowly clambered onto her knees and then her butt so she sat next to Amber. She put a hand on Amber's knee. Amber took Riley's hand.

Then she put her hand on Courtney's belly, careful not to touch the needles there.

"I'm going to close my eyes," Amber said, more to Riley than to anyone else. "See if you can follow where I lead."

Amber didn't look to see if Riley followed. As she sank into Courtney's energy field, rather like plunging into a swimming pool, she felt Riley at her back. Even if the woman didn't see anything, she was there, at least.

With Minnett, looking down into the body at the physical energy fields, Amber always saw in color. Now, she saw only black and white. Even with Stuart, she'd seen in color. It might be that Courtney had no colors left in her body thanks to the frost witch, but Amber had a feeling it was more about her limitations with just Riley backing her up.

The dark fog was still there. It swirled around making the organs hard to see. Amber peered through it. The organs were there, though they seemed slightly smaller than they should be, maybe dried out.

Sinking lower into a deeper level, Amber felt the darkness washing over her. Ice nails flew at her but she dodged them. She heard someone groan, perhaps Riley. Hopefully, she wouldn't be carrying Riley out of there. Amber mentally put up a shield around herself to avoid the little ice nails.

The deep level of Courtney's energetic field was a whirlwind of darkness and ice. Amber had a vague sense of a barren plain around her. Although her physical body remained in the room with Courtney, next to Riley who felt particularly warm, in that realm, a chill ate away at Amber.

She heard nothing, though the whirlwind should have made a sound. She'd not seen anything like it before. It wasn't so active there the other times she'd examined Courtney.

Amber backed out, worried that Courtney would be throwing ice spears into her head, again. This time she wouldn't have Minnett to help so quickly, though someone would call the cat if needed, somehow.

Moving out, the darkness swirled there, too. Looking closer, Amber noted it had entered the organs. If she saw colors, she'd probably see gold or green or red swirled with black or just darken shades of those colors.

Amber moved out of Courtney's body. She felt Riley's head leaning on her shoulder.

"Riley?" Amber said.

Riley groaned. Her body felt too limp. Amber moved her. Kayley had been holding her up.

"What happened?" Amber asked.

"She groaned and then fell to the side," Kayley said. "I was holding her up. She's breathing okay. Doesn't seem particularly distressed except she's unconscious."

Amber looked at Courtney who wasn't looking at them. She had her eyes closed, appearing at peace despite the fact that she'd said she was in pain. Even as Amber thought that a grimace crossed Courtney's face and then smoothed out again.

"Did you notice anything, Courtney?" Amber asked.

"I felt warm. Almost hot. And now I'm cold again," Courtney said. "I heard someone groan. I don't know who. I didn't do anything. I wasn't even in the field."

Amber sighed. Her legs tingled from the way she was sitting. She moved Riley back with Kayley's help. Amber laid her out on the floor.

The door flew open behind her, nearly hitting Riley.

"What have you done?" Stuart demanded. He noted Riley lying on her back. Anastasia was at the door, her gold eyes glaring at everyone in the room. Trag sat behind her. Even Minnett was there, pausing, sniffing the air.

"We were examining Courtney," Amber said. "She's been in more pain than I expected from the needles."

"But we got one of them," Courtney said. Her voice sounded low and crackly as if she'd just woken up from a deep sleep. "And I'll get more."

Then Courtney's voice changed again as she moaned, long and low. She began to snore softly.

*T*he field of dying flowers surrounded her.

Not again.

Courtney wanted to scream but bit back the sound. She'd been able to communicate with Stuart but now that she was alone, or thought she was alone, she stayed silent.

Something else might be out there. With Stuart, she might have faced something else. Alone, she didn't have the will. She'd rather hide.

Looking down, Courtney didn't see her garlic. She walked around, keeping an eye on the ground, noting the way the flower heads tipped to their sides and looked slightly browned or blackened at the edges.

Sniffing the air, she didn't smell her garlic. Nor did she see it as she looked.

Courtney focused on her body, thinking about her hand, which was always the easiest. Nothing happened. A thrill of fear shimmered through her. She couldn't actually say it was in her body because she didn't seem to have a body, but the field of dying flowers got darker. Courtney thought she felt something watching her.

She listened but heard nothing. Not a stray breeze, not the shift of a leaf against another leaf, not the creak of dead leaves under her own feet—not that she had feet.

The silence bothered her. She shut out the field and thought about her body. She focused on the way it had hurt with the needles in, thinking about the pain of the connection, the deep ache that felt as if it had a life of its own. She focused on the smell of garlic, that overwhelming stink that she'd nearly become habituated to.

Courtney thought about bringing her hand up to the wreath and smelling the garlic, in her body. Even if she couldn't feel it, perhaps she'd be able to move her body on her own. Nothing appeared to change. She didn't suddenly feel her body.

Amber had been planning to examine her, again. Courtney had been okay with that. Two other people had been in the room. Courtney had closed her eyes, felt Amber's hand on her belly. She'd felt something zing and join the general ache of the needles. The pain had been sudden. Deep and strong, she'd tensed against it, closing her eyes, trying to will herself not to feel anything.

Then here she was. Maybe she'd willed herself into the field of dying flowers. Courtney tuned out the field and thought about her body. She worked on the feel and the smells. She thought about the sounds of the house.

She felt her body for a moment, the deep ache.

"No you don't," Chase said. She felt him pushing her back.

"Chase?" Courtney said.

"Sort of."

She opened her eyes, saw him. Saw Chase, the way he always looked with his dark hair a little too long—he hadn't had a hair cut in ages—and his big brown eyes. He wore sweats and a plain gray t-shirt. She'd never seen the tee before, but that meant nothing.

"What do you mean sort of?" Courtney asked.

"It's me and it's not. You'll feel better if you give in," Chase said. "There's no way to fight it. Amber certainly doesn't have the ability to get rid of it. She's using needles for god's sake!"

"And they hurt," Courtney said. She didn't add that anything that hurt like that had to be helping. It had to be the frost witch fighting.

"See!" Chase took that as a sign the needles were wrong.

"I want my body back," Courtney said.

"It's better here. You know what we can do? We can grab onto the ice and freeze any of the people we hate. I could freeze this entire house if I wanted to," Chase said. He was smiling. Courtney hadn't ever seen him smile like that. She thought it seemed overdone, perhaps manic.

"You haven't, though," Courtney said.

"I will. I mean they're all looking at you and outside but no one is working on me. Like I don't count or I'm not dangerous. I'm the most dangerous thing here. You know I can reach up through the floors and siphon energy from Stuart? I've been going so slowly that he doesn't even know!" Chase laughed. A bark of a laugh. Not like his easy chuckle.

"What does that get you," Courtney asked, "if you could already freeze everyone, anyway?"

"It keeps me warm," Chase said. "And once he's out of the way, I can freeze the city, probably the state, and take more energy. Then it will all be mine. We won't have to fight to be together anymore. No more of those damned cats!"

Courtney drew back. She and Chase had broken up over his cat Trag. She hadn't wanted the cat, hadn't understood what the cat meant to Chase. The idea that he suddenly wanted to get rid of Trag was unlike the man she knew. And oddly, as she'd lain there in the house, with her garlic and the cats and their people willing to take a chance and help her, she'd become, if not fond of the cats, at least easy with them.

Yet here was Chase, talking about damned cats. Something was wrong.

"No!" Courtney screamed at him, letting out all the fear and anger she was feeling. She wanted her body back. She needed to get away from this creature that was and wasn't Chase.

The force of her scream sent her back to her body. She felt herself falling, like in a dream, and then she was there, in her body, laying on the bed. Amber had left. Everyone was gone. The needles were still in.

Aching pain ranged through her body. Courtney threw her head back and tried to breathe through it. She'd read about breathing through pain. Payton had talked about the importance of breath in her pregnancy and birth classes. Maybe that would help here.

The pain was all-consuming, at once red in her mind and then blue. Courtney held onto it. It was her body and she planned to keep it. She wasn't going to become a thing like Chase.

The door opened. Stuart came back in.

"What happened?" Courtney asked, loosening her jaw enough to speak.

"You threw something Amber describes as ice nails and hit Riley who was backing her up," Stuart said. "Do you not remember?"

"I was back in the field of dying flowers." A sharp pain made her groan at the end of the comment.

"You seemed very able to get back pretty easily when I was there," Stuart said. There was an odd look on his face.

"Chase prevented me from doing it. He said he's been taking energy from you. He said he can freeze the house, the whole household, everyone in it," Courtney said.

"Do you think he can?" Stuart said.

"He said he could. I don't know." Courtney thought about

his question. Did she believe Chase could do what he said? She wasn't sure. He thought he could. She'd been afraid of him, sort of, but she'd also been angry with him. Angry that he didn't look like he was fighting. Maybe he was and that's why nothing was taking over his body.

"Do you think that when I'm in my body, the thing looks like me and talks to Chase?" Courtney asked. The pain was now blue, so pale it might have been white. She didn't try to relax, not wanting to leave Stuart open to attack. He was weak. She knew that. That part of what Chase said was true.

"I don't know," Stuart answered. It was a slow answer. He was thinking about it. Or maybe he was tired.

Stuart left. Courtney lay back on the bed.

Without him as a distraction, the pain threatened to overwhelm her again. She held on, clenching her fists and her jaw. If only she had something to grab. If only Amber would come back and take out the needles.

"*Give in and it will go away,*" Chase's voice whispered in her head.

Courtney refused to give in. No matter what pain there was. She wanted her life back. It might not mean much to anyone, might not look like much, but she had her own dreams. They didn't include destroying the world. There were people she loved, even if Chase wasn't among them any longer.

She had to hold on for Payton, for her mom and her dad, for Payton's baby, for Hannah, even for Wendy at the clinic and Carole, the bitch of a nurse. No matter that she got angry with them for not seeing who she was, they didn't deserve to die.

Courtney held on, groaning and moaning as the pain continued with no end in sight.

DREW

Drew had followed Stuart to the library, where Stuart had stood with the cats. Stuart finally sat down on one of the sofas, eyes half-closed as if listening to music that Drew couldn't hear. Instead of staying and keeping an eye on him, Drew headed down to the first floor.

Tenny had gone to bed. Tom and Fin were in the great room.

"Anything?" Tom asked. "I thought I heard Shahanna once, but she was real distant."

"Stuart thought Courtney could help," Drew said. "Now she knows that we're cut off from the cats." He didn't like that. Stuart was taking a huge risk on her. Stuart, at least, worked for Base Command, which was sort of part of the clowder. Courtney had no ties, not anymore. She'd once dated Chase, but she would always be an outsider in his mind.

"Seemed like she did, a bit," Tom said quietly.

No one was banging on the glass or on the wood, but Drew thought he heard the boards on the deck creak as someone moved. He frowned.

"They're out there," Fin said. He had a cup of coffee in front of him. It smelled good and Drew got up to make himself a cup. He stood by the island, waiting for the coffee, looking over at the table.

"I don't know that she helped enough," Drew said. "I think she could probably do more. Maybe she doesn't want to. Maybe she did this and she wants us to think she's helping us so she can learn more about what we do."

"I think Chase is the person we need to watch out for," Fin said. "He's the one throwing ice around. You had to be unfrozen before you could move yesterday."

"Distraction," Drew said. "I bet Chase does those things so we don't look too closely at Courtney. Notice she didn't come to us between the storms, but only after this snow started, when things got bad."

"I don't know," Tom said. He wasn't even looking at Drew when he spoke. That annoyed him. Drew had felt irritable ever since he'd been unable to hear Mack. The silence in his head was getting to him. Maybe he was irritable because if he wasn't angry, he'd be crying.

His eyes felt warm and Drew went back to thinking about Courtney and the way Stuart had just confided in her. A stupid move. Hadn't Kayley told him he could be a leader? Well, then he needed to tell Stuart that talking to Courtney was stupid.

"Stuart was knocked out," Drew said. His eyes felt more normal, maybe a little dry, but dry was good. "Maybe Courtney got to him then. Maybe she got into his mind. It's not like we know how to check. Amber is hampered because she doesn't have Minnett and even if Minnett sees something, the only person we have to tell us what we saw is Stuart."

Fin gave him a long look. Tom stared at his coffee. That was getting to them. They needed someone else who could verify that Stuart hadn't been taken over. There wasn't any way for them to know he wasn't, not anymore.

"Riley could call Base Command and let them know what happened," Fin said.

"Or I could," Drew said. Normally, guardians didn't call. They left that to healers and researchers, but there wasn't anything in the rules. It was just assumed that guardians would have other things on their plate.

"Or you could," Tom said. "I bet they'd talk more to Riley, though. They have rules about contact and stuff, you know."

"No rules against anyone in the clowder contacting them," Drew said. "It just says it's a better use of manpower to have the researcher do it, or the healer. Mack and I are retired. Good manpower use." Besides, if he was going to act like a leader, a leader was the one who did the calling. In fact, there really wasn't any reason for him to be discussing this with Tom and Fin.

Drew wasn't used to leading. He was used to following what others said, usually the watchers. They were the ones who knew more about what was happening. He'd worked with Matt before retiring. Drew was used to following Matt, but Matt had no ideas. None of them did. Not even Riley, though she kept researching things.

"I wonder what Riley's found out about vampires," Tom said. "The whole garlic thing came from thinking of this frost witch thing as a vampire."

"I haven't seen her," Drew said. "She might have been up late last night." Riley had a tendency to lose track of time when she researched. Then she'd be up at odd hours during the day. After all the banging earlier, he was surprised not to see her downstairs finishing her morning coffee and perhaps some breakfast.

Tom looked back down at his still steaming mug. Fin pulled out a phone and studied it. From downstairs, Drew heard Chase laugh, or perhaps crow was a better term. He'd probably just won a game of pool. Oddly, Drew wasn't feeling his feet tingle any longer. Maybe Chase could only take energy for so long.

Drew left Tom and Fin to their waiting and went downstairs. Anson stood leaning against the wall by the stairwell, arms crossed. Matt and Chase played pool nearby.

The room felt dark, dank, and colder than Drew remembered. Anson had on a hoodie over his shirt.

"What's going on?" Drew asked. No new game had started. In fact, it looked like Matt might be winning the way he was lining up a shot for the eight ball.

"Chase is being weird," Anson said. "I feel like he's doing something and he likes keeping it from us."

"What happens if we find some more garlic for him?" Drew wondered.

Anson raised an eyebrow. "Most the stink came from Tenny's super-garlicked butter she put on that wreath. We could soak something else in it. Maybe a headband or something and fasten it around his neck?"

"I'll go find something," Drew said. They hadn't really worked on Chase since Courtney had wanted the garlic wreath. Amber had wanted to know if it worked. It was possible the garlic would make the creature stronger. No one was around. Drew wanted to see what would happen to Chase if he had that wreath. Worst case, someone could knock him over the head with a pool cue and knock him out.

AMBER

mber and Stuart dragged Riley out of the room, while Kayley kept an eye on Courtney who appeared to go back to sleep after her outburst.

Minnett met them at the door. Amber let the cat do her work, though she worried that something had gotten into Riley and would attack Minnett. Stuart assured Amber that Riley was clear, but Amber didn't understand how he could tell.

Riley came around enough to walk down the stairs to her room. Back on her bed, resting, Amber and Minnett did more healing while Stuart went down to bring up some food. It was early and Riley hadn't had breakfast.

"Something hit me on the head, or that's what it felt like," Riley said.

"What I saw were things that looked like little nails made of ice," Amber said. "What did you see?"

Riley shifted in the bed. Minnett hopped off her belly and started working on her feet, her little claws extended. Riley relaxed a bit more. Amber hoped that Minnett wasn't over-doing it. She found it difficult to watch her cat work when

154

they weren't connected. She'd have no way of knowing if Minnett was in trouble.

"I saw a lot of blackness," Riley said. "There were swirls of shapes but nothing I could make out as more than what I might be imagining, you know?"

Amber nodded. It was too bad. She could have used an extra set of eyes. At least Riley had had her back, though Stuart wasn't pleased with Amber's decision to use her.

Minnett finished. Amber placed her hand over Riley's abdomen, intending to do her own healing and examination.

Riley's organs were colored in shades of gray, though Amber thought maybe she could see a few colors. Amber felt the energy moving through Riley's energetic body a bit more clearly. As she moved in deeper, she saw no darkness, no ice. It wasn't like Chase where she thought there was some even though she couldn't spot it. Hopefully, that meant Riley hadn't been infected.

Stuart came up carrying a bag, which appeared to be how everyone was carrying food, and a large thermos.

"Coffee in the thermos. Cream, no sugar, which is how you take it, I believe." He looked at Riley as he said that.

"Perfect." Riley struggled to sit up in her bed. She pushed herself up until she was leaning against pillows back against the headboard.

Stuart set the food down on a narrow dresser which served as a nightstand. "I also brought up some of those toaster pastries, a muffin, and two of the breakfast sandwiches that were in the freezer. The sugar will help perk you up more quickly."

Riley nodded. She took the cup he'd brought with the thermos and poured some coffee out. Then she started on one of the breakfast sandwiches, which had been placed carefully in a glass food storage container, the sides steamed from the heat of their contents.

"I understand why you did this," Stuart said, looking over at Amber, "but what you did was dangerous. If something had happened to both of you, we'd have had no one to work energetically."

"And it's okay if you and I are injured?" Amber asked, crossing her arms. Her stomach growled at the smell of the food. The pastry she'd had earlier seemed like a very long time ago.

"Base Command will replace me," Stuart said. "Riley and Kayley could take over for you at least until Base Command sent another healer. They'd probably pull someone with seniority from another clowder. If both of you are gone, there would only be Minnett and Kayley and no way for them to communicate, considering the telepathic links are still blocked."

"Did you get through to Trag?" Amber asked.

"I can hear him when he's close to me," Stuart said.

"I feel like we need to work on Chase," Riley said, finishing the first sandwich. She picked up one of the toaster pastries. She offered the muffin to Amber. "Not a big fan of blueberry."

Amber took it gratefully. She tried to not wolf it down.

"Why?" Stuart asked.

"I just kept thinking of him while I was out. Like he was around. You know that sense you get when you've closed your eyes and you know someone is there? I was expecting it to be him though I never saw anyone." Riley finished the pastry only slightly before Amber finished the muffin.

Stuart nodded. "Then maybe we do need to look at him. I worry that without the telepathic link, we won't be able to do the work we need to. And if Courtney is that dangerous, he could be even more so."

"Why are you so sure that Courtney's on our side?"

Amber asked. "Maybe she's the one directing all this and I just can't see it without Minnett."

"I went to her field of dying flowers," Stuart said. "It's a raw place. She sounded scared but also like she was willing to fight. She helped me out of there which she didn't need to do. Neither Minnett nor I detect any sort of infection or possession from my time with her, either."

Amber turned over the words. Raw. Like Courtney was stripped bare, yet she was helpful. It wasn't the memory she'd have of the entitled little girl who had visited the clowder with Chase once, back when they were dating. She'd hated the cats. It surprised Amber that Courtney would turn to them for assistance, even.

"I'm going to go down and get some food," Amber said. "And feed Minnett. She's clearly been doing a lot of healing."

Minnett gave a tiny mew. Unusual for her to use a cat voice like that, out loud, but they had no other way to communicate. Amber wondered how Minnett knew exactly what she was thinking.

Leaving the room, Amber paused by the door, looking back at the cat who leaped off the bed and ran down the stairs, leaving Amber to follow. Anastasia was already leaping on the bed to take her place next to Riley.

Watching the cat hurry to the kitchen, Amber thought she would have to make sure Minnett knew not to be on the first floor when she and Stuart examined Chase. She had no idea what would happen but for some reason, she dreaded what was coming.

STUART

Stuart watched Amber leave the room. Riley settled back to finish her food and coffee. Anastasia washed her belly while Riley ate. While they couldn't hear them, the cats were making sure their people were okay. Or as much as they could without the link. He followed Amber downstairs, a few moments after, thoughtful.

Trag sat at the top of the stairs and looked down. Something down there clearly had his attention.

Stuart sniffed the air but smelled nothing other than the coffee he'd brought up a few minutes ago.

"*What?*" Stuart thought at the cat.

"*Something is building. I can feel it,*" Trag said. "*The others can, too. Minnett doesn't like being downstairs. She wants to come up.*"

Mack hurried by them, tail down. Unusual in one of the guardian cats.

"*Is it Chase?*" Stuart asked.

"*It comes from below, so perhaps.*" If Trag sounded sad, Stuart didn't pick the emotion up telepathically. Cats often got very depressed when their humans died, refusing for months to do their work. They always got a break. Trag was getting no such break though his loss was every bit as great. Seeing Chase daily, not being able to contact him, knowing what was going on, Stuart could only imagine that was worse.

"What about from above? From Courtney?" Stuart asked.

"There are fluctuations in energy up there. Fluctuations happen all the time. We can feel it. What is happening downstairs is different. I feel as if I'm waiting for an attack." Trag's fur looked slightly raised.

Stuart headed down the stairs. Trag looked at him, started to stand. Stuart went back and asked him to stay. They didn't need to lose one of the guardian cats even if Chase was lost.

Cats didn't normally look relieved but Trag seemed to, though Stuart could not have said why. He laid a hand on the banister and continued down to the first floor. Minnett was eating, though she seemed skittish, jumping a bit when Stuart entered the room.

Amber stood near the island making breakfast. Eggs and sausage. Their delicious scent starting to cover the overly strong garlic smell from last night.

"Something is happening," Stuart said. "I think it's best if Minnett went upstairs, sooner rather than later."

Amber frowned. "What is it? Should I not have breakfast?"

"Eat," Stuart said, "but be ready."

Tom stared at him from his place at the table. Fin put away his phone and stood up, stretching. He looked towards the boarded-up windows and then away, practically placing an ear against them lest people come through the boards.

Downstairs.

Where Chase was.

Anson had pulled the hurricane shutters across the big basement room. Those would be harder to break through.

Stuart didn't think the threat came from outside. What Trag wasn't saying, didn't want to admit, was that the danger came from Chase.

"Where's Drew?" Stuart asked. Normally Drew was dogging Stuart's steps and, if not his, Amber's.

"He found an old sweatband of mine and dunked it in garlic butter and is planning to make Chase wear it," Fin said. "Why?"

Stuart didn't like the idea of Drew and Chase. "I'll be downstairs. Come down after you finish," Stuart told Amber.

He tried not to hurry too much as he went down the stairs. He didn't want to appear worried or scared. Drew might be following his own hunch. It could be a good one.

Chase stood by the pool table, but he wasn't wearing the sweatband. The garlic drenched band rested on a small round table off to one side. Drew stood beside Chase.

Too close to Chase.

Stuart watched as Drew gestured towards the band.

Matt stood off to the side, behind Drew, where he could keep an eye on things. He held a pool cue, every muscle ready to use it as a weapon if it came to that.

"What's going on?" Stuart asked, walking forward. The aroma of garlic wafted towards him, making him want to gag.

"He thinks I'm going to wear that thing." Chase pointed to the table.

Stuart didn't have to ask what he was referring to. He knew.

"And he's refusing," Drew said. "I think Courtney might have been right. The garlic works."

"It only works if you believe and I don't," Chase said. "I just don't want to walk around smelling like a pizza. That thing will get it in my hair. Bad enough that Courtney stinks of it on her body and her clothing."

Drew didn't back down.

He also didn't ask the question that was first in Stuart's mind: How did Chase know what Courtney smelled like?

It could be a guess. It could be that Drew had said something about the wreath and Chase inferred from there.

It could be something more.

No one moved. No one said anything.

The hairs on Stuart's neck raised. He wanted to turn and look behind him, though he knew no one was there.

Power wafted from Chase, a slimy, filthy power that made Stuart want to turn and run. Chase would use that power if he could.

He was waiting for something, but Stuart had no idea what that something was.

Stuart knew of only one way to stop him: they needed Chase unconscious.

The clowder medic room was well equipped for anything they could need when dealing with an unusual injury. It included antibiotics, painkillers, and tranquilizers. Stuart slipped into the room, flipping on lights that felt too bright after the dimness of the main room.

The pharmacy was well labeled and locked. Anyone purchasing certain classes of drugs could be audited. Stuart had a feeling that Base Command made it unlikely that a clowder would turn up on an auditor's sheet, but all the same, Amber had one locked cabinet. Stuart didn't have the keys.

Any drugs that would knock Chase out would be in that cabinet. He needed the keys. Stuart left the room.

Drew still stood a little too close to Chase. Chase didn't seem bothered at all. In fact, he appeared to be almost smiling.

Matt's position hadn't changed either. If anything he looked even more ready to swing the cue.

Stuart hurried up the stairs to talk to Amber about sedating Chase. They could restrain him.

The real Chase would understand.

This Chase…

Stuart had a feeling they were going to have a fight on their hands.

No one came back for her. Courtney waited. She listened for Kayley outside the door. The needles still hurt, but not quite like they had. She drifted into a light doze, and found herself on a dock near a lake, one so large you could barely see the far shore. The day was gray and overcast and a light breeze made Courtney shiver.

A broad sandy beach met the water which looked too dark to Courtney's eye, probably because of the cloud cover. Trees hovered in the background.

"Hey," Chase said. He was on a little jet boat which sat low in the water, the paint a shiny royal blue, a single white racing stripe down the side. The four seats were covered in matte white faux-leather, or maybe real leather, though Courtney didn't know why you'd put real leather in a boat.

"Hey yourself," Courtney said. She moved closer to Chase. He leaned back. Courtney sniffed. Smelled garlic. She looked around the beach, searching for someone eating pizza but she was alone on the dock, but for Chase and his boat.

Courtney felt scared for some reason.

"Get in," Chase said.

"No." Courtney didn't want to go in the boat. The depths of the lake made it look black in the dim light, small waves breaking white against the dark water. She shivered, wishing she'd worn heavier clothing.

"Come on. You know you will," Chase said. "It's the only way out of here. Don't you want to leave?"

Courtney looked back. Instead of a broad sandy beach, she saw only dead flowers. These weren't even her dying flowers, but dead carnations and roses. Black petals lay strewn around instead of sand. The edges of each petal looked sharp. The trees beyond had grown to become menacing monsters, their broad limbs reaching out to grab her, the breeze that chilled her making them move enough that she stepped back towards Chase's boat.

"That's it," Chase said. He put a hand on her, sending a chill deep into her body almost as if he were made of ice.

"No." Courtney pulled away from him.

Chunks of ice floated on the black water. Something swam beneath the ice, something big. It was only a shadow, there for a minute, but Courtney wanted to run screaming from the dock. No safety awaited on the lake…or in the boat.

"What? You're going to try and navigate those trees?" Chase asked.

Courtney didn't look back at him, but walked along the dock. The thin soles of her shoes let her feet feel every sharp edge of every worn and splintered board. As the bottoms of her feet began to feel wet, she knew they bled.

Not looking down or back. Courtney hurried into the forest, her heart hammering. The trees threw long shadows across the petal beach. The sharp edges lanced deeply through her shoes and into her skin. Pain shot up her legs.

The pain reminded Courtney of the acupuncture treatment Amber had been giving her. She was dreaming. It wasn't the field of dying flowers.

"I can take you there." A woman appeared before her, long blonde hair, lithe, perfectly proportioned body. She wore a long white gown that billowed far too easily in the slight breeze. Blue veins showed through her thin pale skin. While beautiful, Courtney didn't trust her any more than she trusted Chase.

"No." Courtney wasn't going anywhere with this woman. Chase might have been part of a nightmare, but not this woman. Courtney's skin crawled even in the dream. She felt the pulse of her heart like a drumbeat throughout her body. A deep ache reached her from every single point of the needles.

Courtney drew in a breath, smelling the garlic. She wanted garlic there with her to throw at this vampire creature.

In her hand, a large bulb appeared. Courtney held it out to the woman. The vampire woman shrank back, her skin becoming even thinner and paler until she looked like a medical model with clear plastic showing off the muscles and organs inside.

Courtney held onto the garlic. The smell made her cough. As she did so, she expelled a dark cloud from inside her. It flowed around the dream, flowing back to the woman with the transparent skin.

"Leave me alone," Courtney said. No more coughing. She hoped that she'd gotten rid of the entity she'd carried. Moving through the forest, which remained dark but didn't seem as menacing as it had, Courtney had hope.

Breaking through the last of the branches, she stood on the edge of the field of dying flowers. Courtney thought about her body. She pulled herself towards her body, like a climber on a rope, pulling with all her might to get back to reality.

Then she opened her eyes, looked at the room around

her. The light felt different. No one had come to move or change the needles. She still lay there, feeling the ache. Once again, she marveled at how much less the needles made her hurt.

"Kayley?" Courtney called.

Kayley cracked open the door but she didn't cross the threshold. Courtney didn't exactly blame her, but she wanted someone to take the needles out.

"Can someone take the needles out?" Courtney asked. She felt as if she were done with them.

"I'll see what I can do," Kayley said, closing the door again.

Courtney leaned back to wait, hoping it wouldn't be too long before someone came.

She closed her eyes for a moment. The door banged open against the wall. Opening her eyes, Courtney expected Stuart and Amber, perhaps angry with her for asking to have the needles removed.

Instead, Chase loomed in the doorway.

Courtney screamed.

The basement smelled unusually damp and, despite trying to make her brain compensate for the shutters across the windows, too dark. Amber noted that Matt and Drew scowled at Chase, no longer pretending to play pool. Chase had his chest puffed out like he was about to hit Drew, but he never raised a hand. Their voices were low enough that Amber couldn't hear what was said.

Drew took a half step back, but continued to stare at Chase as if daring him to hit him.

Amber didn't like the tension but she had no idea how to diffuse it. Instead, she scuttled towards her office until she noticed the medic room door open.

Stuart was inside, looking around. The cabinet that held the restricted medications was open, but Amber was glad to see that the glass case inside was undamaged and the drugs appeared to be there.

"What's going on?" she asked, walking into the room. The light in there was bright against the creamy floors and walls.

"I want to sedate Chase. Drew came down with a sweatband doused in garlic butter, but Chase won't wear it. I'm not sure I blame him." Stuart continued looking at the cabinet.

"I'll find the key," Amber said, "but you'll have to explain how we're going to do this."

Stuart watched while Amber went to her office. She pulled the key from the central drawer in her desk. The only label was a bright red key tag on it with no writing. Easy enough to find for anyone who knew what to look for. That was good for the clowder. Not so good if anyone ever stole something and they were audited.

Back in the medic room, Amber opened the cabinet and stared. "How under do you want him?" she asked.

"As under as we can get him without killing him. If he's the reason we can't hear the cats— and I suspect he might be —I want him as out as possible. Trag is examining the barriers. I'm hoping that if we can lower them even for a short time, the cats will understand how they work and be able to work around them. We might have periodic cuts in communication but it will come back sooner than it is this time."

Amber nodded. It was a good idea. "I have Courtney upstairs with needles. Maybe we should start by knocking her out."

"When Courtney relaxes and gets knocked out, the entity in her appears to take over," Stuart said. "I'm curious if the same thing happens with Chase. However, I am counting on a bit of disorientation with the drugs. The entity may be less affected, but the medications are going to affect the physical body, perhaps slowing it down."

Amber couldn't fault his ideas. Hopefully, whatever entity possessed Courtney wouldn't take that moment to come out. She didn't know how they'd work against both Chase and Courtney at the same time.

Drawing up a syringe full of tranquilizers, the strongest they had, Amber set it down on the counter.

"I'm going to see if I can get Chase in here for an examination. It wouldn't be unheard of," Amber said.

She walked out into the other room, immediately aware of the tension. While it wasn't directed at her, it thrummed through her body. She walked stiffly through the room, her mouth dry. Given a choice, Amber would have turned and run.

"Chase," she said. Her voice wasn't loud but it cut through the room like a gunshot as all three men turned to look at her.

"What?" Chase asked. He had that stupid, smug smile on his face. Everything normal. Nothing to see.

"I want to examine you while it's snowing." Amber gestured to the medic room.

"Or while Courtney is here? Is Stuart going to look for links between us?" Chase smirked.

"Perhaps," Amber said. She didn't drop her gaze. Something in his eyes told her that would be a very bad idea.

Chase continued to stare at her. Amber's stomach turned. While she'd needed to eat, she regretted breakfast, earlier. Then, Chase looked away and he sauntered around Drew, hitting him with his shoulder.

Drew had to step back to keep his balance.

Chase didn't acknowledge hitting Drew. Drew might as well not have been there at all.

Amber let Chase precede her to the medic room. The idea of him following behind her made her skin crawl. Chase had no such issues. Even seeing Stuart in the room, Chase hopped up on the nearest table and laid back. He didn't bother with taking off his shoes.

"I assume I can stay dressed as this is just an examination, right?" Chase asked. "Where's the cat?"

"She won't be helping," Amber said. She wanted Minnett nowhere near Chase.

"Too bad. I won't be able to kill her painlessly. She'll have to hurt like the rest." Chase said it all so normally as if discussing what to watch on television.

Chills ran down Amber's spine. Minnett wouldn't be anywhere near Chase until they all ascertained that he was free of the entity inside him.

Amber wondered when Chase had stopped being Chase and became this other thing. Before, he had been Chase, if a little weird. Now, to voice the things he was saying, she didn't believe there was anything left of the man she'd worked with.

Drew came into the room. Stuart nodded at him to come in further. Drew didn't quite touch Chase, but he was ready to hold him down. Amber picked up the syringe. She put it back down, thinking better of it. She dug through the cupboards until she found the restraints.

She held them low, coming around from the head of the table so it was harder for Chase to see. She passed one to Stuart and one to Drew.

Amber placed a hand on Chase's belly like she was going to start the exam. She wanted him focused on her and what she was doing. She half-closed her eyes, letting herself sink into Chase's energetic body.

Her senses went on alert the moment she sank down. Something was wrong. The organs all looked normal. They were more brightly colored than Courtney's. Amber looked closer at his kidneys—they were closest to where she'd entered. Shiny black, they looked in perfect condition, almost too pristine.

Amber moved up to the liver. The green color of the liver appeared every bit as beautiful as the first leaves of spring. No darkness there. Amber moved up Chase's spine. Last time, there had been shadows hiding in the spinal column, but now Chase's body was clear.

Alone, with only Riley as backup, Amber had seen Courtney in black and white. This couldn't be what Chase's internal organs looked like.

Amber started sinking deeper but Chase began to fight. Pulling out of her light trance, she opened her eyes.

Stuart and Drew had restraints on his arms. Chase kicked his legs back and forth. While she was examining Chase, Matt had come into the room and was already at the far cabinet where the restraints were kept, pulling out a pair for Chase's legs. Drew and Stuart did their best to hold Chase down.

"You tricked me," Chase snarled. "Whatever you think you're going to do, you won't succeed." Spittle flew from his mouth.

Amber stepped over to Chase's feet. She let Matt fasten the restraints at the foot of the table. When he finished, she held down a foot while Matt wrapped the heavy leather around the ankle and fastened it. Then they moved to the other foot.

Chase was fighting so hard, Amber couldn't hold him still. Drew moved to the foot and held it down so Matt could work. Amber went to the counter to grab the syringe.

"Ready?" she asked Stuart.

He nodded.

Chase looked over at her. "You won't find anything. You never do. You're an idiot." He looked away as Amber inserted the syringe into a vein, almost expertly, and injected him.

Nothing worked immediately. Chase screamed some threats. His words started to slur and his head moved to the side.

"Think he's faking?" Drew asked.

Amber wondered the same thing. She didn't know the drugs well enough to know how long it would take to knock him out.

"I didn't see anything earlier. In fact, he looks too healthy," Amber said. "I'm going back in."

"Let me join you," Stuart said, holding out a hand.

Together, Amber led him down into Chase's energetic body. At first, she just saw the bright colors of the organs, each of them in perfect health. She felt Stuart behind her. The movement felt as if he were removing cobwebs. As he did so, Amber noted the thick dark tendrils running through all of Chase's organs. Up close, they appeared like dark stitches against the organs as if something had ripped Chase apart and sewn him up again.

Amber swallowed hard. She had no idea how to fix that. She dove deeper into the energetic plain. Like Courtney, the plain was darkness. Ice flew around up there, but rather than needles, it fell as hail, the ice bouncing around her feet.

Here and there, Amber saw lightning bolts hitting the ground, frozen in time. Stuart went up to one and knocked it aside. The bolt danced around like a snake, sending Amber falling back from it. Stuart hit another of them. The same thing happened.

She imagined a large sword. She started cutting away at the lightning bolts hitting the earth. She worked until her arms got tired, though they were imaginary. Clearly, she'd worked far harder than she thought she ought to.

Amber looked around at the darkened plain. More light shone, letting her see further than just an arm's length ahead. Lightning bolts still reached the earth but they were further away. She needed rest. Stuart probably did, too.

She pulled both of them out, nearly losing her balance when she came out of the trance.

Stuart stumbled as well and hit the table behind them before managing to steady himself.

"You were under nearly half an hour," Drew said. "Are you okay?"

Chase still slept.

"*You appear to have cleared the blockages*," Minnett said, telepathically.

Thrilled, Amber sent about a hundred messages to the cat, overwhelming the link with everything she wanted to know and felt Minnett needed to know.

Matt's face was more relaxed than it had been. Even Drew seemed calmer. Stuart smiled a bit.

"Trag said that everyone started getting their links back over the last half an hour," Stuart said, interrupting the sharing Amber was doing with Minnett.

"*I believe that you were clearing all sorts of links. The creature in Chase was siphoning energy from the telepathic links. That was the blockage we felt. Apparently, even our communications are energy for this creature.*" Minnett sounded fascinated by the idea.

"I don't know how to clear everything from Chase's body," Amber said. "It's like this thing has merged into his organs. Courtney's organs are just black. Chase's look normal but for the stitching I saw around them. Like he'd been destroyed and sewn back up."

She hated saying it. It felt like saying Chase himself was destroyed, but she'd seen nothing of him on the energetic plane.

"His energetic patterns are slightly shifted from the last time we examined him, before the snow," Stuart said. "It's similar but not quite the same. There's enough of Chase there to attempt to fool someone not looking too closely."

"How do we keep him from cutting off the telepathic links?" Amber asked.

Stuart looked thoughtful.

"*We know it was eating the energy*," Minnett said. "*We can't not use energy to communicate but Base Command is considering ways to make other energy resources more enticing.*"

"Other energy resources?" Amber asked.

"Emotions play a role. The entity appears to like it when people get mad. We've noticed that before and the pattern is continuing. Also, it can feed directly upon a person. Stuart cut a link to himself that Chase was apparently feasting on for some time. He should be able to work more efficiently, now." Minnett's voice began to get fuzzy.

Chase shook his head back and forth.

"He's coming around and interfering with the bonds," Amber said.

"Let's try the sweatband," Drew said. He went out to the other room and was back in a few moments with the garlic soaked sweatband. He didn't slip it over Chase's head but he put it near his neck, where the fumes, already strong enough to make Amber step back, would be right under his nose.

Chase coughed a few times.

"You need to get to Courtney," Minnett said. *"Something has happened."*

Amber lingered with Chase for a second.

"Go. Now." Minnett ordered.

Amber glanced at Stuart. He was already leaving.

"Stay with him," Amber told Drew and Matt. "Don't let him up." She hurried from the room to get to Courtney.

Stuart hurried out of the medic room the moment Trag told him Courtney was screaming. Having the telepathic bond back made him feel powerful. Of course, Trag told him Minnett felt that the entity in Chase had been siphoning off energy from him and that link had been severed. Perhaps he felt so good because that drain was gone.

Reaching the first floor, Stuart saw Tom near the stairs, looking towards the upper floors. A woman's screams reached Stuart's ears even as Tom moved out of the way and Stuart bounded up to the second floor.

Hardly winded he hurried up to the third floor, barely acknowledging that Riley had poked her head out of her doorway to see what was happening. Kayley had opened the door to Courtney's room but was standing back a few feet. Cari came out of the room next door in pajama bottoms and a t-shirt, her feet in tennis shoes, ready for a fight.

Kayley turned as Stuart reached Cari's door. Cari must have been on the night shift and had been trying to sleep.

Stuart got to the door and looked in. Courtney was alone in the room, but she was moving from side to side on the bed, screaming. He walked in, slowly, looking around. He let his vision go unfocused and looked around for anything in the energetic realm.

Vague shapes reached him. Perhaps human or humanoid, but he couldn't get a fix on them. It was like looking at clear glass underwater. He knew they were there, but couldn't quite see them.

He heard Amber breathing hard behind him, having stepped into the room.

She jogged over to Courtney, putting her hands on Courtney's shoulders. "Courtney!" Amber called.

Courtney's screams slowed but didn't quite stop. Like a baby having a tantrum.

Courtney struggled against Amber. Amber sighed and began to pull needles out.

The vague shapes flowed back to Courtney. Water flowing downstream.

Courtney's screams quieted further.

"Don't pull any more needles," Stuart said.

"It's been over an hour," Amber replied. "I shouldn't leave them in longer. We'll try again tomorrow."

Stuart didn't know if there'd be a tomorrow but something in Amber's voice suggested she wasn't going to argue with him about the medicine. She knew this stuff. He didn't.

"*Minnett is telling her your observations,*" Trag assured him. "*She still believes it's best if the needles come out for now. Perhaps another day Courtney will be better able to fight off whatever happened this afternoon.*"

"I saw Chase. Here. I thought it was you, come to take out the needles for me, but it was Chase. He was coming for me," Courtney said. Her left hand, the hand closest to Amber held onto the garlic wreath she wore as a necklace.

Stuart coughed a little, the stink a bit too strong for him

now that he wasn't concentrating on something else. He remained back a bit from Courtney.

"Did he leave or is he still here?" Stuart asked.

"I woke up?" Courtney said. "That's what it felt like."

Stuart didn't think that's all that had happened. The entity inside her could still play her while she rested. He had hoped she'd be an ally for them, perhaps help them a bit, but the frost witch was clearly able to control her, even if its control was based in subtle manipulation.

Stuart backed out of the room, leaving Amber to minister to a now silent Courtney. He almost tripped on Cari who was standing by the door.

"Sorry," Cari said, moving aside.

Stuart turned around walked into the hallway. Kayley closed the door.

"Did you notice anything unusual in the room?" Stuart asked both of them, once they were out of easy ear-shout of Courtney.

"Other than Courtney screaming for no reason?" Kayley asked.

"Other than that, yes," Stuart confirmed.

Kayley shook her head. "It felt cold in there, colder than the rest of the house. I don't know if that's normal for this room?"

Cari shook her head. "It's not. Julia and I store stuff in here, mostly in the closet, and it's not normally a cold room."

"So there's that," Kayley said. "And the garlic smell but that's not unusual given what she's wearing."

Stuart nodded. "Are there other things vampires hate that don't stink up the house?"

"Silver," Cari said. "And crosses."

"Sunlight," Kayley supplied.

"Wooden stakes to the heart," Cari added, "although if

you're thinking of using it on Courtney, that probably isn't where I'd start."

"Mirrors," Kayley said. "Holy water, but like crosses, I don't know that that applies here."

Stuart nodded. "There are mirrors around. Has Courtney had a problem looking in them?"

Cari shrugged. "I haven't noticed a problem."

"She hasn't screamed going into the bathroom and there's a huge mirror in there," Kayley said. The vanity in the adjoining bathroom was as long as the tub and shower combo and had a flat mirror over the entire thing. It made the small room look larger. It would be impossible to just avoid looking at it unless Courtney had put up a sheet to cover it.

"Sunlight?" Stuart asked.

"It's cloudy. No one really knows how much sunlight will harm a vampire," Kayley said.

"Silver would be the next thing I'd try, if anyone has any real silver. It's hard to know. Does silver-plate count or does it have to be solid?" Cari chewed on her thumb.

"And do they need to be bullets?" Kayley asked.

"She's not a werewolf. I think silver bullets are for them," Cari corrected her.

Although, Stuart thought, if they shot her in the leg with a silver bullet it might work. It would certainly slow her down. What would silver in her system do?

He opened the door to reenter Courtney's room. Amber was still with her. They were talking about the experience with the needles. He peeked into the bathroom. The mirror was uncovered, the lights off.

"How are you?" Stuart asked her, coming over towards the bed. He paused a few feet away. He could understand why vampires might not like garlic. In bulk, as it was around Courtney's neck, it was certainly overpowering.

"Okay, I guess," Courtney said. "It's not gone, though, is it? Maybe you should throw me through that portal or whatever like you did with those jars of gunk." She referred to the jars in which Amber had placed shadows she'd found in the bodies of those she'd examined during the last snow.

"Those were sent to a place where nothing lives," Stuart said. "Doing so would kill you."

"Maybe that's what you need to do," Courtney told him. She said it simply as if discussing whether they needed to give her a haircut.

"I have no desire to kill you. Especially not like that." Stuart watched to see what she'd say.

"You can't try and kill me here, not like with a knife or a bullet. I feel like that would make the creature jump to someone else, someone new. I know what's going on. I'm hanging on as much as I can, hoping this thing will die but it's not dying. I think it might be trying to get out, maybe get to someone else, or worse, get to Chase."

"Why do you think that?" Stuart asked.

"It's not fighting as hard to make me relax. I mean, it sort of hurt Riley but not like I hurt Amber. The needles are doing something but I'm afraid it's just going to push the entity out of my body and into someone new. You have to help me defeat it or else I have to die." Courtney's voice held conviction, certainty that she was right.

It wasn't that Stuart thought she was wrong. He just didn't know how to help her defeat the entity, as she put it. And he was not yet ready to think about murdering this healthy young woman.

Because that's what it would be if he sent her out through the portal.

Murder.

DREW

Chase took turns glaring at Drew and Matt after Amber left. Drew noticed the slight flexing of Chase's lower arm muscles as he tested the strength of the caramel-colored restraints. They'd held Chase during the last snow, so Drew wasn't terribly worried.

Still, Amber had told him to stay there, to make sure Chase didn't get up, as if she thought he might be able to. Drew crossed his arms and watched. Matt moved back a few feet to the table just beyond Chase's and sat, legs swinging. Neither of them said anything.

"What's been going on?" Drew asked Mack.

The telepathic link was back but not quite as good as normal. He felt as if there were static on the line. Mack didn't break up and disappear but he was harder to hear. While Drew had found distance made a difference the time he'd visited family in Michigan, it hadn't made this much of a difference. Mack's voice had been softer, but not filled with static.

"All of us are on the second floor, except Minnett who is up on the third, near the stairs," Mack said. *"We are working on ways to*

circumvent whatever it is that Chase did to cut off the telepathic link."

"Chase is gone. You can't save him," Chase said, or the thing in Chase said, interrupting Drew's conversation with Mack. Drew didn't doubt that human Chase was probably unconscious, in his equivalent of the field that Courtney went to when she was unconscious. If he trusted Courtney at all, he'd send her to the field to try and pull Chase out like she did with Stuart.

"*What would happen if Chase and Courtney met up?*" Mack asked. Drew felt something else behind the question, something the cat was hiding from him. It wasn't well hidden. Drew thought that Mack would let him know why in a few minutes.

"*Not sure,*" Drew thought back to the cat. He often talked out loud to Mack. Everyone spoke to their bond-mates out loud from time to time. The sounds of odd half-conversations would float through the clowder house on a regular basis, or they had until everyone had been cut off.

"Nothing," Chase said, grinning at Drew. "I know what the cat wanted. And he's going to die, like all of them."

Drew felt a shudder from Mack. "*As we thought,*" Mack said. "*He's still lightly linked to the telepathic connection. He's not completely diverting the energy of it right now, but he can hear what we know and communicate.*"

"I am more powerful than you tiny creatures can fathom," Chase announced. He looked first at Matt, who had stopped swinging his legs and looked ready to punch Chase, and then at Drew.

Drew said nothing. He forced himself not to take a step back from the table. He needed to be there, ready to move, to intercept should Chase make good on his promises. The entity kept threatening things, but rarely did them. No one had died. Not yet.

Chase smiled. He raised a hand, with all the ease of someone lifting a fork from the table and the restraint ripped apart. Matt was already springing into action.

Drew felt the purring start upstairs, the sound of feline magic.

Pounding started on the walls outside, a thundering ring against the hurricane shutters, a sound that Drew felt deep in his bones.

He wasn't aware of having moved, but he was holding down Chase's arm. Chase's legs were free, though Drew hadn't heard anything rip, not that he could hear over the pounding and thundering sounds.

The purring calmed him slightly, kept him in the fight. He felt stronger than he had.

Matt let go of Chase's arm and threw a punch.

It connected with Chase's chin, tipping his slightly raised head up and back.

Chase fell back, stilled for a second.

The pounding paused.

Then, Chase sat up, a movement even more fluid than when Stuart sat up from lying down. Drew had noticed that gravity didn't seem to hold the Base Command human in quite the same way it held normal people or even bond-mates.

Drew tried to push Chase down but a cannonball of ice threw him back towards the doorway.

His back hit the door, the wood splintering. A shard of wood from the door pierced his side.

Warm fluid trickled down towards his feet even as he kept falling, now off to the side of the door.

Laying on his back on the floor in the doorway, Drew tried to get his breath.

His vision went in and out.

Cold made it hard to take in a deep breath. When he breathed out, his breath fogged the air.

He'd barely had time to notice when Fin stood over him, bo-stick at hand, protecting him.

The garlic headband landed near Drew. The garlic felt uncommonly warm as if it had absorbed all the heat in the room.

Matt screamed, a single, strangled cry.

Another blast hit Drew. It wasn't cold, exactly. It was as if someone had started sucking all the heat from his body.

Drew felt the warmth leave. Felt it being pulled him.

He tried to roll over, rolling into Fin, who was also rolling away trying to get out of the blast area.

It was so hard to move, even to roll.

The cold made his limbs heavy, made it hard to think and breathe.

Drew had to pause and rest, his mind beginning to go dark.

"Move!" Mack screamed in his head.

Drew tried. Didn't know if he succeeded.

Through the thundering pounding that had started back up, the cats purring surrounded him, softened the injuries he'd sustained. Kept him calm rather than panicking that he was dying.

ourtney felt something pulling at her. It felt as if someone had a rope tied around her intestines and was trying to pull them through her lower back. The pulling became an ache. Her body temperature dropped.

Courtney bit back another scream. They'd think she was crazy. She couldn't stop the moan, though.

Amber placed a hand on her forehead before drawing back. "What is it?"

Courtney forced her eyes open, despite the pain. Amber was shaking Courtney's hand, rubbing it against her body. Amber's fingers looked purple. Touching Courtney had given Amber frostbite.

Shivering, Courtney felt herself getting angry. She'd done what she could to fight the vampire. Amber had been using needles to fight her way. Between the two of them, they should have done something. Courtney knew the snow still fell outside. She hadn't looked out a window but knew it was falling harder.

Banging and thundering came from around the house.

"Shit," Amber muttered. "They're back."

Neighbors, then, banging on the walls. They'd done that before and stopped. Stuart had made them stop but he'd ended up in the field of dying flowers. Courtney wondered if she needed to go back there to rescue him.

"*Yes…*" a small voice whispered, deep in her mind.

The entity lied. Courtney knew that, though she also felt the pull to make sure he wasn't there. The entity inside her wanted her gone. She had to hang onto consciousness.

She sat up, despite the pain. She didn't want to close her eyes, fearing that might bring her to the field of dying flowers. She needed to focus on something, though. Had to figure out what was going on with this pain, this chill.

Amber tried to force her to lie back down. Courtney pushed her away. Heard Amber fall. Courtney had pushed her harder than she intended. The entity clearly added strength to her body.

Even angrier now, her head pounded with the sound of the banging, Courtney let the heat of her anger warm her. She found the trail of cold inside her, let her imagination follow it.

An icy snake-like thing was hanging on her low back. Courtney imagined taking a hatchet and cutting it off. An eerie scream echoed in her mind.

Between her anger and the fact that nothing was trying to siphon her energy for the moment, Courtney felt stronger.

She took a moment to focus on the room, looking around, making sure she was there and not in some weird dream.

Amber sat near the door, holding her head. "What the hell?" she asked, glaring at Courtney.

"Sorry," Courtney said. She meant it. Kayley opened the door, perhaps warned by the cats.

Courtney walked towards the young woman. Kayley drew herself up, preparing to fight. Courtney knew before anything happened that Kayley would use some sort of eastern fighting style like karate. It wasn't karate, though. Courtney almost tasted the name on her tongue before it was gone.

It didn't matter. Kayley couldn't hurt her. The only person who could hurt her was Chase. He would if they didn't let her take care of him first.

"I need to get to Chase," Courtney said. "He started this."

"I can't let you do that," Kayley said. She moved to force Courtney back to the bed.

Courtney thrust her arm out at an angle, grabbing and twisting Kayley's arm. The unexpected move had Kayley off balance. Courtney didn't break Kayley's arm, though she felt the pressure she applied to Kayley's bone. It was enough to hurt the young woman, but not quite break her arm.

Courtney had never known things like this before. She didn't understand why she knew them now, but she had to get to Chase before he destroyed everyone.

She felt Drew around her. The big guy was scared and alone. Chase had gone after him hard, much harder than Courtney had gone after Amber or Kayley.

She stepped around Kayley, moving faster so that the young woman couldn't try and stop her again. Courtney didn't want to injure her further.

The banging was louder in the hallway. Beneath the banging was a loud purr. The cats. The sound irritated her, crawling up her back. As she got closer to the stairs, Courtney felt her power dissipating. Her legs got heavy. She had to push herself down to the second floor, fighting through fatigue.

It wasn't Chase this time. It was the purring spell.

"I'm trying to help," Courtney screamed, adding to the cacophony around her.

Stuart stepped in front of her before she was able to start down the stairs to the first floor. He wasn't completely in front of the stairs. Courtney thought about pushing herself around him, but felt the magic that he had and the fatigue in her limbs. She wouldn't make it. Still, she had to get to the basement.

"Let me go," Courtney said. "I need to get down there. I can help. I think Drew is dying."

"Mack is also afraid he's dying," Stuart said. "How do I know you won't join Chase?"

"You don't," Courtney said. "I don't. But I know the entity wanted me to go to sleep. It didn't want me awake. I have to try."

"I can't let you," Stuart said. He moved towards her.

Courtney held out a hand. She didn't think about ice. She didn't want to send a blast of ice through Stuart. Instead, she wanted a shield around herself.

A wall of ice rose up between them.

"I have to try," Courtney said. Her voice sounded firm even to her. She'd never talked like that, always raising the ends of her sentences into questions.

Stuart felt the ice, his hands becoming pale from the chill. Courtney saw rivulets of water running down the wall where he touched. Her wall wouldn't hold him long.

Stuart noticed the changes, too. Courtney hurried as much as she was able around the bend to the stairs to the first floor.

"If you try and stop me, will you have enough magic to stop Chase?" Courtney called back behind her.

Stuart paused where he was, still behind the wall which hadn't yet melted into the carpet. Courtney didn't look back.

Tom and Tenny were at the bottom of the stairs.

Someone else was in the great room. It smelled, to her, like Anson. Courtney wondered if she shouldn't go back to the upstairs room, keep the power away from Chase. She'd never had the ability to tell who was who by smell. Not until today.

Thumps came from the basement.

Courtney envisioned an ice bubble around her that would follow her as she walked. Ice built up around her, just beyond her nose, and made a nice oval that ended at the ground, just wide enough for a normal stride.

Courtney passed by Tom and Tenny. They banged on the ice shield. The ice began to leak water as it started to melt from their body heat, but it didn't break.

Anson used a crowbar against the shield. It bounced off, though Courtney noted the star-shaped cracks that radiated out from where it hit. Eventually, the shield would shatter.

She hurried down the stairs, leaving Anson and the others to follow, or not. Movement was easier now.

Courtney reached the basement. Her nose twitched at the damp scent. The banging hurt her ears. She wanted to cover her ears with her hands and close her eyes against the onslaught.

Fin was lying on his side against the pool table. A foot twitched. Drew wasn't moving at all. Courtney saw fog around his body.

Julia was lying in a heap a few feet from the stairwell. Something moved behind the pool table. Courtney knew it was Cari.

In the middle of everything, holding a pool cue, was Chase.

"Courtney! You came to join me?"

"Never!" Courtney yelled. She sent a blast of cold at him. Cari ducked when she saw Courtney put her hands up.

Chase raised a hand grabbed the icy cloud and pulled it to

him. He smiled. "I'm more powerful than you!" he sang, a little kid teasing a big sister.

Courtney's shield began to melt faster. Chase half-closed his eyes and smiled. He wiggled his tongue just outside his lips, mimicking drinking.

Ice worked for him. He really was far more powerful than she was. She'd made a mistake. A huge mistake coming down to the basement, thinking she could fight him. Nothing could stand against him.

Anger burned through her. Courtney held onto it. This creature ate life force.

Courtney thought of rain. Showers that didn't freeze, didn't heat too much either because those things could be used. Swampy rain.

At first, nothing happened when she raised her hands, thinking about it. Then, as if someone had installed a sprinkler system in the basement, Courtney let muddy rain fall on Chase.

He frowned, not certain what to do with the rain. He shook it off. Then he worked on freezing it. Courtney saw the energy coming to him as he drained the heat out of the water, turning it to ice. It was cool enough that he used more energy draining the heat than he got back.

She smiled, making it rain harder. The pool table was already a lost cause. Courtney saw places where Chase had set up traps to catch energy anytime someone walked on the floor above. She severed them, all with a smile.

Chase was still draining the heat from the rain she made fall. He didn't notice he was losing energy.

Puddles formed on the floor where the carpet could no longer soak up any more water. The pounding stopped outside.

She pulled Julia up, turning her so that her face was up and she wouldn't drown. Chase was between her and Fin.

She couldn't help him. She hoped the water didn't rise too far. It wasn't raining that hard.

Courtney let the rain cool a little further, so that it was just warm enough to fall as rain and not as sleet or hail.

Chase continued to pull what energy he could out of it. Now he losing energy even faster. Courtney hoped she could tire him out.

Something must have shown on her face because he stopped pulling energy abruptly. He put out a hand to her.

Courtney felt something twist her guts, again. She closed her eyes against the pain. Mentally, she searched for the link and cut it. This time, Courtney imagined holding onto the link, like it was a hose.

She pulled it towards her.

Courtney opened her eyes. Chase looked worried. His eyes closed slightly.

Courtney pulled on the hose harder, drawing it to herself. Something slimy touched her hand. She let dropped it, shoved it away from her.

Chase's eyes opened wider. He frowned at her, made like he was going to swear.

Cari rose up behind him and hit him over the head with a pool cue.

Courtney didn't think it would do anything. She prepared to do what she could to save Cari. But Chase dropped straight down into a pile not far from Fin.

Courtney's jaw dropped wondering what kind of a game he was playing. Water fell on her tongue. She held up a hand to stop the rain.

Silence echoed in the basement. Too much silence. Distantly, she heard purring. Her heart was beating too fast. She didn't think it could pound that hard if she ran a marathon. Heat flashed through her body. Not angry heat, just heat. The next moment she shivered with cold.

Courtney backed up to the step. She needed to find out what was happening with Drew. If he wasn't dead, he was close.

She didn't think she had the strength to help him, though. Her head dropped. She felt the world receding but she determinedly hung onto consciousness. Who knew what would happen if she lost control of her body and the entity took over.

AMBER

Amber had been standing over Courtney when Courtney had pushed her back. Amber hadn't expected to go flying. Courtney's hand had shot up from her side and it had appeared as if she'd barely touch Amber, just enough to get her to move back, a polite ask. Instead, the pressure had been harder than expected, and Amber had landed on her butt on the floor.

The room grew colder around her as if the window had been opened, allowing the freezing temperatures outside to flow in. As far as Amber could tell, the window was still closed. She didn't feel a draft, just cold that came at her from all directions, holding her in an icy embrace.

Amber had barely gotten her bearings when Kayley went falling backward as well. Courtney had knocked Kayley down with no apparent effort.

"What the hell?" Kayley asked. "Were we wrong about her?"

"I don't know," Amber said quietly.

She pushed herself up, a more difficult movement than she would have expected. The joints on her lower body groaned with the effort. The freeze seemed to hold her immobile. Kayley, too, had difficulties, but once they were both up, Kayley ran down the hallway towards Courtney.

Amber hurried after her as well, but she didn't run. She heard the cats purring downstairs. Minnett would be there amongst the others. She would be focused on whatever magic they were sending. Given the way Amber's body loosened up, it was a spell to calm and put someone to sleep. Perhaps she'd find Courtney near the library, where she knew the cats had gathered, curled on the floor, asleep.

The pounding on the stairs suggested otherwise. Whatever was going on, no doubt Amber would be needed, so she continued hurrying. Minnett wouldn't be able to easily break concentration to give her any information. Amber would have to find a human for that.

On the second floor, she found Stuart with Kayley. Water pooled on the carpet.

"What?" Amber asked.

While the air had been warmer than in Courtney's room, now she felt a chill that came from the space between Stuart and Kayley. In fact, when she tried to focus on Stuart, she felt as if she were peering at him underwater.

"She put up a wall of ice to keep me from following her," Stuart said. "I don't believe she means to injure us. In fact, I think she hopes to do battle with Chase. The wall is melting but I doubt I'll get there in time to help."

Kayley looked back at Amber. "Do you think she's really helping?"

Amber shrugged. "She could have killed both of us if that was her plan. She didn't act like she was trying to knock us over at all."

"She made sure to put me behind a wall. My telepathic link to Trag and to Essalyn at Base Command are both intact," Stuart said. "If you have any protection magic, I'd use it for the people down there."

Riley appeared in her doorway. Normally, Riley would have been in the library with the cats. Gray shadows still pulled at her eyes and her face was far too pale. She stood half bent-over. Still recovering from helping Amber try and heal Courtney.

"I don't know if we can trust her. What if the creature wants us alive to siphon energy?" Riley asked. "Chase's entity took energy from the telepathic bond. We might be more valuable alive."

"That's certainly possible," Stuart said. It wasn't lost on Amber that he didn't like that possible motivation. "I think our first priority would be to help knock Chase out—really knock him out. Then take care of Courtney if need be."

Kayley was already half-way down the stairs to the first floor. Amber hurried after. Her shoulder brushed the ice wall and sent a spike of frigid pain through her body. Biting back a gasp, she ran to catch up with Kayley.

The banging on the shutters echoed through the first floor so loudly that Amber felt it in her bones. She didn't know how Tenny and Tom stood it while they guarded the first floor.

Amber had nearly reached the top of the basement stairs when the sounds suddenly stopped. The silence hurt her ears nearly as badly as the banging.

"What do you suppose happened?" Tenny asked, her voice barely above a whisper.

The air filled with the tension of waiting. Tenny's muscles were taut, ready to fight against whatever came next. Tom appeared equally ready to meet yet another threat, though the sounds themselves weren't a threat but merely a distraction and annoyance. What if the people outside had been paving the way for something else?

Anson stood as if frozen, holding a crowbar. Amber practically saw his ears straining against the silence. Waiting.

After a few breaths, Amber continued on down the stairs. Tom, Anson, and Tenny would have to hold the fort up there. If they were lucky, Stuart would get down in time to help.

Amber reached the bottom of the stairs in time to see Kayley step off the lower step, where she'd been waiting. As she watched, Cari hit Chase over the head with a pool cue.

Courtney turned towards the medic room but slumped down before she took a second step.

"Tie him up," Amber ordered Cari. No one needed to ask who she wanted tied up. "As tight as you can."

Amber stepped on to the basement floor, surprised at all the water, practically a flood. Her feet tingled and quickly went numb. Fin lay in the water along with Julia. Julia had been turned so that she wouldn't breathe in any water. She must be freezing, though.

Kayley was helping Cari. Amber went to Fin, to see if he was breathing. He was. She propped him up against the back of the pool table. His head hung down against his chest. Best she could do for the moment.

Behind her, Courtney was slumped over. Amber saw her chest rise and fall. Unconscious but alive.

Drew lay on his back. She didn't see his chest moving.

Amber ran to him. Put her fingers on his neck, hoping to find a pulse. Nothing.

"I need the defibrillator!" Amber yelled.

"Tenny is coming down," Minnett said. At nearly the same time, Tenny came hurrying down the stairs. A squish when she hit the damp carpeting which had already soaked up the water that covered it just moments ago.

Amber started chest compressions on Drew. She needed to get him up out of the water. She wished Tom had come.

"He's in the water," Tenny said. "Let me help."

Tenny was stronger than Amber would have thought. Together they were able to pull Drew into the medic room. The water had come into the room nearest the door, just a small puddle as if someone had opened an outside door against a hard rain.

Pulling him up onto the table where Chase had been earlier was more difficult. Drew's arms flopped around and nearly had him flopping back onto the floor. It Tenny hadn't been helping, there was no way Amber would have gotten him up there.

Once he was situated, Amber went back to compressions until Tenny returned with the defibrillator.

She noticed, with half her mind that Matt lay on his side in the medic room. Amber thought he was breathing but she couldn't break off compressions to be certain.

Tenny tore the shirt from Drew's chest. The defibrillator was automated so anyone trained could use it, and Amber had made sure they were all trained. She'd never expected any of them would have to use it, not even herself. While Tenny set up the machine, Amber did a few more compressions.

"Clear!" Tenny called.

Amber stopped and backed up.

Tenny placed the paddles on Drew's chest. Amber watched his body rise and fall back down. Tenny looked at the monitor on the box.

"Anything?" Amber asked. She hurried over to the pharmacy, digging around, looking for adrenaline. In an emergency that might help restart his heart.

"Nothing."

"Again!" Amber ordered, not even looking back. They couldn't lose Drew.

Amber heard a cat scream. The pain brought tears to her eyes though the sound came from upstairs. Again.

"Mack?" Amber thought to Minnett.

The little tuxie appeared in the doorway. *"Mack is sure he's gone,"* Minnett said. *"Has been since we started purring, but Mack did his duty."*

"Anything?" Amber asked Tenny having heard the second zap.

"Nothing," Tenny said.

Amber filled the syringe, tears filling her eyes. Since the cats started purring was a long time to be down.

Minnett was standing on Drew now. Tenny couldn't shock him again. Amber felt the cat searching through his energetic body. Grayness surrounded her. Minnett sunk deeper.

Amber jabbed the syringe into Drew's chest. She pounded on it, feeling the ribs crack. Good. She was working hard enough.

Minnett sat next to her working. Amber felt the emptiness of the energetic plain.

"I can't..." Minnett said and backed out. She didn't finish. Just leaped to the floor and began to yowl along with Mack.

Tenny set the paddles down and bent over the table.

Matt groaned from his place on the floor as if the sorrow had woken him.

Amber covered her mouth. She backed up to feel the wall behind her. She'd not expected to lose a patient. She was an acupuncturist, not an emergency room doctor. Who would have expected...

This?

Kayley came in, holding Julia up. The two of them bumped together, Julia hanging her head.

The pain that radiated from the cat's yowl made Courtney wince. Her legs shook when she pushed herself up. She knew there were others behind her, working on Fin, making sure Chase stayed unconscious.

Having worked with the magic, Courtney could feel it running through her. She was powerful beyond her wildest dreams. Part of her wanted to catch her breath and run through the streets punishing those who annoyed her and randomly rewarding those she might like. Except that would be wrong.

The ideas of what she could do floated through her mind. Many of them made her stomach churn until it hurt. The entity was still there, still attempting to guide her.

It reveled in the pain the clowder was feeling over losing Drew.

Courtney leaned against the wall and stepped into the medic room.

Kayley had set Julia on the far table. Drew lay on the first table, his shirt torn, his large, creamy white chest open to the chill in the room. Courtney noted Amber's little tuxedo cat laying beside the door with her front feet out in front of her, head up at an awkward angle, moaning and yowling with the others from upstairs.

Tears formed in the corners of Courtney's eyes. How could you not love a creature that mourned its people like that?

It hurt her to be in the room with all that pain. Courtney had to lean against the doorframe to hold herself up. Amber was leaning against the counter, staring at the top of Drew's head, her eyes slightly dilated. Courtney wasn't sure Amber saw him at all.

Courtney raised a hand, sent a blast of cold air towards Drew and the table. Ice crystals formed on the table, on Drew. When he was covered in white, Courtney let her hand fall.

"Why?" Tenny asked, her head coming up. Her eyes narrowed, her muscles tensed, ready to spring at Courtney.

"I might be able to save him, but not now. Freezing will keep everything as it is," Courtney said. She felt her legs giving way. Even the blast of cold had been too much. She was worn out.

Her stomach growled. She longed for food. The entity longed for life force. She felt it reaching out to grab energy from Amber, Tenny, Julia, Minnett. It loved their pain, wanted to devour it.

If she thought it would ease the anguish they were feeling, Courtney would have let the entity at it. Instead, she put it in a cage in her mind, twining imaginary garlic around the bars, keeping it at bay. Her hands went to her own wreath of garlic, the smell finally reaching her again.

"What do you mean?" Amber demanded taking a step forward.

Courtney took a few breaths, listening to more steps

hurrying down to the basement. She felt Stuart there, knew he'd be on her side.

"I think I can let the entity soak up energy, from all of you, from the people outside, too. I think when I'm rested I can put that energy into Drew. Bring him back," Courtney said. She thought. It wasn't exact. She didn't know who Drew would be when he came back. Would he be an entity made real or would he be the person these people loved? Would his soul be drawn back once it had energy?

"When you're rested?" Amber snapped.

Courtney didn't like her tone. As if she didn't deserve to rest. She'd kept Chase from killing others, she knew it. Had felt the desire in him. The entity in him was tired of being underestimated. It felt strong and powerful and ready to begin taking over. It had grown.

"Would he still be Drew?" Tenny asked quietly.

Kayley stared. Courtney saw the longing in her eyes, felt the entity banging the cage, wanting to feed on that longing.

"I don't know," Courtney said. "He could be Drew. He could be something else. He could even be another entity. I don't think that last will happen because the entity in me doesn't like the idea. It likes that you're hurting. It wants to feed on that sorrow. It's locked away for now."

"Can you know that it hasn't learned that the best way to manipulate you is by making you think it doesn't want something?" Stuart's voice came from behind her. Courtney heard the carefully neutral tones in it.

"I don't," Courtney said. She felt herself slipping further down the wall. Her body ached and her eyes wanted to close. "And I'm barely holding on to consciousness. I don't know what will happen if I fall asleep and rest."

Courtney felt Stuart putting magic on her, a sort of holding magic around her body. It was weak and puny, though he may have once thought it powerful. It would hold as well as a flimsy locked door against a determined burglar, but it would buy them some time to wake her.

"Someone needs to wake me if it seems like anything is happening. The cats should be able to tell." If they weren't so focused on Mack's sorrow, that is. She had to hope.

Courtney's legs gave way and she swam into darkness. As it closed over her, she felt pleased that she wasn't immediately thrust into the field of dying flowers.

STUART

Stuart felt as if there were too many voices in his head. Trag's distress communicated itself telepathically. He not only heard the cat joining in with the song upstairs but he felt the pain they were all feeling. Mack was inconsolable. Though Trag was aware of Courtney's offer, Mack didn't trust her, not now. Not for this.

None of the bond-mate cats could allow themselves to hope for Drew's resurrection.

Essalyn, at Base Command, was equally distressed, though her distress was tempered by the fact that she saw Drew as less useful than other human bond-mates. Questions flew at Stuart from Essalyn, probably put to her via Base Command. Most he didn't have answers to. Even the ones he could answer, Stuart couldn't form thoughts as quickly as the questions besieged him.

The stress tore at him. He wanted to focus on what Courtney had suggested.

"Do you trust her?" Essalyn asked.

Stuart didn't know. He trusted that she'd try. He wasn't

sure she was savvy enough to know whether she was being played. If they let her siphon energy from them to bring Drew back would the entity infect Drew? Worse, with Drew dead for so long, would he be able to fight for his body? Essentially they could be creating the very monster they wanted to destroy.

"The safe play is to leave the bond-mate dead and have your mourning. Then toss Courtney and Chase through the portal," Essalyn said.

"I don't think we're ready to lose another bond-mate," Stuart thought back at her.

"Would you rather lose the whole clowder? If you bet on her and she fails, you could end up doing that." The suggestion was likely not coming from Essalyn herself. Stuart felt a sort of distaste for the comment as if Essalyn might have argued, but was required to pass on the information.

Of course, he didn't want to lose the entire clowder. Nor did he wish to lose his own life.

He didn't see letting Courtney and Chase die right then as the right move. Courtney, especially, could be a help. If there were other people infected or possessed like she was, they needed someone like her who could help them. It was a risk, but sometimes the greatest risks offered the greatest rewards.

Besides, Stuart didn't think he could possibly convince the clowder to give up on Drew now that Courtney had planted the seed that she might be able to resurrect him.

"Let's get Matt, Fin, and Julia taken care of," Stuart said. He tried to block out Trag's pain. He'd forgotten how difficult it was to not feel what one's bond-mate felt. Even with the more limited connection he had with Trag, emotions flowed through the link as if they were one.

Julia laid back down. Stuart went and helped Cari with Fin. They'd made it only a few steps before Fin had fallen again. It could have been pain or weakness or the grief he was feeling through his telepathic link.

When the three of them got Fin situated, Stuart noted Amber working on Julia. Hopefully, Julia wouldn't need much healing.

Matt was propped up against the side of the table. His head lolled but at least he was able to hold himself up, a little.

Tenny stood over Courtney, keeping a careful eye on her.

"Anson is out with Chase. What do we do with him?" Cari asked after they settled Fin on the table. She went to take Julia's hand.

Stuart didn't know. Essalyn said Base Command was ready to send him through a portal. Stuart felt a flair of anger at their lack of caring. It came from Trag. All the cats in the clowder would know that Base Command wanted to get rid of Chase. While none of them trusted Chase, Trag was still half-grieving the loss of his bond-mate. The cats hadn't given up on him yet. The fact that Base Command had, hurt them all.

Chase had broken through the restraints in the medic room. The lower portion of the restraints dangled from the table Drew lay on. Nothing said Chase couldn't break through a wall. If he were strong enough to rip through the leather, he could bang his way through the drywall of his room.

"The storage room behind the hallway is all cement," Kayley said, practically reading his mind. Or perhaps Trag had passed on his thoughts to the clowder.

"We have chains in the garage, too," Tenny said.

"Anson knows how to weld well enough," Kayley added.

Stuart nodded. "I'll watch Courtney. I have the best chance of seeing energetic changes that suggest she's waking. Tenny, you tell Anson what's going on, what we need, and then get the chains. Kayley can find the welding tools."

"What's outside?" Stuart asked Trag.

"The people are still milling around," Trag answered. At least the cats were still watching.

They couldn't spare anyone else. Stuart knelt down by Courtney, wishing there was a bed for her down there. No way could he carry her up the stairs to the third floor.

Behind him, he heard Amber move to Fin's bed. He bowed his head in thought, knowing they had decisions to discuss when Courtney woke. He wasn't sure if he hoped she'd wake soon or not. More time would give him more time to think, but he doubted that if he pondered this question for a hundred years that he'd have a good answer.

His heart, what was left of it, reminded him that they had to try everything. It meant keeping Courtney alive. It meant chaining Chase in the storage room, hoping it could hold him. It meant allowing Courtney to try reviving Drew.

COURTNEY

Courtney slept deeply without dreams. When she swam to wakefulness, still feeling exhaustion weighing down her limbs, she was met by the entity fighting to get out of its cage. Courtney ignored it. Stuart sat next to her and he watched her surface.

Her neck ached. Her back hurt. She couldn't feel her butt at all. "How long?" Courtney asked.

"About four hours," Stuart said.

Courtney pushed herself up. She was no longer physically weak. She didn't have as much power as she had had before. She'd gain more with food and more rest. If she siphoned life force from everyone around her, she'd gain even more.

"Is it okay if I go upstairs, eat, and maybe get real sleep?" Courtney asked. She didn't know what she'd do if he said no.

Stuart didn't and the two of them walked up to the kitchen. Tom was in the great room. He looked up when he saw them.

"Snow has stopped," he said.

Apparently, she'd managed to weaken the entity, again. Perhaps when she'd started draining Chase's power and cutting off his easy access to more life force. Courtney didn't know if Chase was fighting for them, too, or if the entity had completely destroyed the person she knew as Chase.

She ate whatever Stuart put in front of her. She knew if he'd put a raw egg in front of her she wouldn't have bothered to cook it. She'd have eaten it like that. Her body was famished. Tom's life energy drew her. She wanted to suck that down as quickly as she sucked down the food. Instead, Courtney made her way to the third floor. She practically passed out when she reached the bed.

When she woke, she didn't remember laying down. Once again the sleep had been dreamless. She was hungry but not famished.

The entity still rattled the cage she'd created. Sitting up, Courtney noticed Stuart sitting on the floor near the door. He appeared to be dozing. She looked outside. The sky was pinkish-blue. Dusk, then, though it looked wrong. Perhaps an after-effect of becoming so used to clouds and grayness.

"It's morning," Stuart said, "not evening." Courtney wondered if he read her mind. No wonder he was dozing if it were morning.

"No wonder I'm hungry again," Courtney said.

Stuart nodded. "Chase woke. He can't quite break the chains. No one is in the room with him. The cats are aware that he'll try to siphon energy. We've created a circle around him to warn us if he manages it."

Courtney nodded. It wouldn't be unlike the circle Stuart had created around her. Completely breakable but not without warning those watching it. In time the entity would learn ways around it, but they had weeks, perhaps months before that happened. Chase's entity wouldn't learn any faster than the one inside her.

"Fin, Julia, and Matt?" Courtney asked.

"Matt was fine, just knocked out for a moment. Fin and

Julia just needed food and rest. Minnett and Amber gave them some energy."

"After everyone eats breakfast, I'll start grabbing energy," Courtney said. "I feel strong enough to work on Drew. Unless…?"

"The clowder thinks we need to try," Stuart said.

Courtney sensed words not spoken. The clowder might have decided but there'd been plenty of arguments.

Stuart left her, so she showered, which refreshed her further. Courtney caught herself siphoning energy from the water. It wasn't much but it helped. While it strengthened the entity, she didn't care right at that moment. She was going to need its power soon enough.

She and Stuart made a huge breakfast. Enough for everyone. The smells drew Fin from his room on the first floor. The cats came down and Stuart fed them, as well. They all looked listless. Mack, Drew's huge orange tabby looked smaller now. He ate a few bites and then returned to a small space between the cat tree and the fireplace, which, for once, was off.

Courtney felt sorrow wafting off of the cat. She avoided siphoning it. It wouldn't help him feel less. It would just make him less resilient against the feelings. She was going to need to be careful about what she took from the rest of the clowder.

Eventually, the smells of food brought everyone to the kitchen. Julia and Cari took over the cooking. Pancakes with frozen blueberries, heavy on the syrup. More than a dozen eggs scrambled with vegetables and cheese, bacon, and sausage. Someone found muffins and they all ate those. The toaster was also pressed into use until no one could eat another bite.

Courtney finished her fourth pancake. She half-closed her eyes to sense the energies around her. It was a little like seeing the flowers in the field of dying flowers. The healthier they were, the perkier the red flower. These flowers were rich and red. Ready. Her fingers itched to reach out and pluck them.

Courtney knew the impulse was that of the entity. She couldn't just pluck the flowers. She needed to slowly sip nectar from each one.

The image of a hummingbird reached her. Courtney flitted from one flower to the next, sipping. The flower turned darkish brown at the edges and began to wilt. She moved to the next until she'd drunk as much as she could from each of the flowers.

She opened her eyes. Everyone at the table looked tired. Normal people would have said food coma after the meal.

"You were siphoning energy, weren't you?" Stuart asked.

Courtney nodded. "Too much?"

"I think a bit. Not fatal, but I expect we'll be eating the muffins again shortly."

"I need more," she said.

"We don't have it to give."

Courtney stood up. She went to the front door. No one stopped her. No one had the energy to stop her even if they wanted to. She opened the door, not fearing the people who might be outside. She had more than enough energy to freeze them where they stood. It would kill them, but it would keep the clowder safe, at least for a time.

No one milled around. They'd gone home for the night. Courtney stepped out into the bright sunlight. The entity in her disliked it. She fought an urge to run back to the shadows of the house. Vampires again.

She took a long whiff of the garlic wreath around her neck and pushed on. She reached out with her mind. The people next door were still sleeping. She started siphoning energy from them.

Across the street, she felt a child having a tantrum. She took that energy, too. He'd be quiet for a while. She had no idea if he'd be more prone to tantrums after this or not. Perhaps for a short time.

She pulled energy from the parents, too, and even the large poodle the people had. Courtney was particularly careful with the dog. Animals didn't have as much life force and tended to give it almost willingly.

She pulled back before injuring anyone. She felt ready.

The entity in her was greedy for more, wanting her to explore the limits of how far she could siphon energy and how much she could hold at one time. Courtney had to force herself to stop, to walk back inside—at least the entity liked that—and tell Stuart she was ready.

Amber and Stuart both went downstairs with her. Courtney felt Chase in the storage room. She felt the longing from him for the life force she currently held. The longing pleased her entity which wanted to feed on that one. Courtney let it do so, just a bit.

Once in the medic room, she needed to unfreeze Drew. The temperature in there was cool but not cold. He was already beginning to thaw despite Courtney's work. She breathed out quickly, letting warmth flow from her.

She saw no change in his body, though the soft drips falling to the floor started falling faster.

Courtney drew in three more breaths. She attempted to center herself. It had been easy fighting Chase. She'd just done whatever was needed to defend herself and the house. She'd had to play with what she could and couldn't do to harm him the most, but the how of it had been instinctual. While she knew what was possible in terms of filling Drew with life force, she wasn't quite sure what to do next.

Amber stood next to the table ready. Stuart stood behind

Courtney, perhaps to knock her out if she did something she shouldn't.

Courtney closed her eyes. She imagined a long hose joining her to Drew. She let the life force she'd drawn flow through the hose into Drew. The entity wanted to flow along with the hose.

Courtney held onto the creature.

In her mind's eye, the entity looked at first like a large fish out of water, its tail beating against her imaginary hands, hoping to slide into the flow. Then it changed to an eel-like creature with long sharp teeth that tried to sink into her imaginary hands.

Courtney imaged steel gloves on her fingers, preventing the damage.

It became a bird, a large creature like a chicken but with a beak like a parrot. It tried to grab onto the gloves with that beak, tried to flutter its wings, anything to get away from Courtney.

Courtney heard a groan and closed off the flow of life force. She opened her eyes.

Amber was working over Drew. Stuart was helping. Courtney felt Minnett come into the room, the cat's energy brighter than anyone else's.

She stood back, suddenly proud of what she'd done. For the first time in a long time, she felt almost peaceful about her life.

DREW

It hurt to breathe. Actually, Drew had to think about how to breathe, as if somehow he'd forgotten. His body ached everywhere. And he was cold. Too cold. Like someone had laid him on a slab of ice.

"*Mack?*" he thought.

No response.

He tried opening his eyes. He felt his eyelids but couldn't pry them open. His first thought was that someone had glued them shut, though why anyone would do that was beyond him. He tried raising an arm. That worked but he felt like his arm was weighted down in concrete.

He let his attention fade out into blackness, not even having the energy to wonder what had happened to him.

The next thing he knew he was awake, again. Aware. Still in pain.

"*Mack?*" he tried again.

Still no response.

This time he heard noises. People talking.

He was still cold but there was warmth beneath his back.

His eyelids opened slowly. They felt sticky, like peeling

212

open the flap on an envelope, but this time, at least they opened.

"You're awake," Amber said.

Drew opened his mouth to ask what had happened. Couldn't get a sound out.

"Don't try and talk," Amber told him. He had to try, had to find out what happened to Mack. He couldn't hear him.

"Mack's okay," the voice was Courtney's. She was there with him. Drew frowned. She was infected with the frost witch. They needed to take care of her, but she was sitting there in the room with him as if she were the doctor. Fear leaked into the confusion in his mind.

How did she know how Mack was?

"It's okay," Amber said. "Courtney's right. Mack's okay. I expect he'll have to reform the bond with you soon."

Drew didn't understand what was happening. He didn't hurt quite so much as he got warmer. Whatever Amber was doing, there was heat everywhere now. He could even breathe more deeply.

He closed his eyes again. He worried about trusting Courtney in the room alone with Amber—was she alone?— but he didn't have the strength to do anything about it, not right then. His stomach growled.

He wondered when his last meal had been. He vaguely remembered the last snow, remembered Courtney at the house. Remembered Chase threatening them all.

"*Useless...*" the thought passed through his mind, said in Chase's voice.

Drew pushed it away. A memory.

"*I can help you not be useless,*" Chase said. Except it was like talking to Mack. Telepathic thoughts. But these were in Chase's voice.

"*See how powerful I am now?*" Chase told him. "*I can help you. We need to stop Courtney. She'll destroy everything. It's her plan. I've been hiding, letting her think I can't do much. She can't know about me."*

"What's happened?" Drew asked.

"I'll tell you. Just fall asleep and I'll make sure you know everything when you wake up," Chase said. *"And I'll be sure to let you know how to help stop Courtney from hurting everyone."*

Drew drifted off into strange dreams that he only half understood.

Amber was gone when he woke, but Stuart was there.

"How do you feel?" Stuart asked him.

"More awake," Drew croaked, happy he had a voice at all. He hadn't before.

Stuart nodded and leaned back against the table behind him, continuing to watch. Drew didn't understand why they were watching him. They ought to be watching Courtney. He wanted to rush upstairs and take care of her, but he knew he couldn't do that, not yet. There were things he didn't understand.

"How's Chase?" Drew asked.

If Stuart was surprised by his question he didn't show it.

"We have him taken care of, for now."

Drew thought the term was interesting. Chase was taken care of. Maybe the dreams he'd had were right. Courtney had tried to hurt everyone, but Chase had stopped her, barely.

"Chase helped me," Drew muttered.

Something flickered across Stuart's face. He looked as if he didn't know what to say. Drew wondered if he had it wrong or maybe Stuart was working with Courtney. In his dream, Chase had told him she was a master at manipulating and you couldn't trust what she said.

Maybe things looked different to the others. Maybe he was wrong and Chase was manipulating him. Drew turned his head, hoping to fall back to sleep but his body was awake now, calling for food.

"I'm hungry," he told Stuart.

That made Stuart smile. The smile pleased Drew. He needed to talk to someone about what happened but he had no idea who to trust, particularly since he couldn't hear Mack. He wished he understood more about what had happened.

Amber did checks on Drew multiple times a day. After three days she let him go back to his room. Minnett told her Mack wanted to reconnect with him, but Trag kept saying Drew smelled like Chase so the cats held off. Even Mack stepped warily around him.

In her office, with Drew back upstairs, Amber sat with Stuart.

"Drew's energy patterns are not the same," Stuart said. "I don't like that. Base Command doesn't like that. But at the same time, he was dead for over a day. How could the patterns be the same?"

"He has some shadows in his energetic field. It's like what I saw in Matt when he came back from outside during the first snow," Amber said. "I clean them out, but they reappear. That's not like Matt. I'm not sure where the shadows are coming from. It's more than I ever saw in Chase."

Stuart nodded. "And in Courtney everything is black."

"It's moving dark water, now," Amber corrected. "I see spots of light but…"

"She's more infected than Drew," Stuart finished.

"As far as I can see. But I can't see anything in Chase and from what Matt, Fin, and Julia say, Chase was the one who started things. He gave Drew a zap that killed him and he didn't even have to breathe hard. The only reason he was out was because Courtney stopped him," Amber said. "I can't see her endgame if she's not really helping us."

"Base Command is discussing sending someone from Cat Home here. They'll come through this portal if they arrive," Stuart said.

"Is that a good thing or not?" Amber asked.

Stuart shrugged.

Amber didn't know what the shrug meant. He was closed-mouthed about what he knew about Cat Home. She didn't even know what the creatures looked like there. Were they giant cats? Normal-sized cats? Humanoid?

Asking would get her nowhere. Stuart would only shrug and say nothing.

"I don't believe he knows," Minnett said. *"Trag has been able to see some secrets wiped from our minds by Base Command. I have the impression that the creatures on Cat Home are shapeshifters."*

Amber had a sudden flash on a series of something called Shifter Romance that a girlfriend used to love to read.

"Not that sort of shifter," Minnett said. *"Not a werewolf or whatever. Cat Home natives can merely take whatever shape they desire."*

If they came, Amber hoped they took a shape that didn't scare the crap out of her. The idea of them already did. She worried, too, that they'd expect her to be able to heal Chase and, perhaps, Drew if he were infected. She'd been the most vocal about letting him stay dead.

Being a healer, everyone had thought she'd want him saved no matter what. Amber might not want to be responsible for his death, but in her world, the dead stayed dead. That didn't need to change. She'd been overruled by Stuart and the rest of the clowder. Kayley had been conflicted, not certain that Drew would have wanted them to bring him back, not with the risk.

Mack had actually concurred with Kayley. Unfortunately, no one knew for certain what Drew would want or how he'd be if they brought him back.

It had been decided that morale would be better if they tried. They left unspoken the fact that someone would have to kill him again if it wasn't actually Drew.

Amber let it go. She was a healer, not a killer. That job would go to someone else, perhaps Courtney as she was likely the only one strong enough. Unless the creature from Cat Home was as powerful as Courtney was.

"Courtney is learning how to keep the entity inside her, as she calls it, at bay," Stuart said. "I've been teaching her some meditation tricks. She picks them up easily."

Courtney was no longer wearing garlic around her neck but kept a few bulbs in her pockets, pulling them out now and then to take a deep whiff. It was better for the rest of the household than the stupid necklace.

Amber and Stuart went on to discuss the energy patterns of everyone in the household. Amber knew Stuart wondered how long she and Minnett could keep up working as hard as they were. She didn't know either. Hopefully, when the creature from Cat Home came, if it came, that would change.

COURTNEY

Once again, Courtney felt like she was waiting. Waiting for the other shoe to drop, for something to happen. Instead of being in her little house, she was in the clowder. Stuart was teaching her meditation techniques to help her stay in control.

The snow had melted into slush and then slowly cleared as the temperatures warmed into something close to normal. The clouds hovered, always off to the edge of the city as if waiting to be invited back in. Courtney knew that sooner or later they would come.

She felt Chase getting stronger in his storage room prison. His energy felt like a snake slithering around the house, searching out the unwary to siphon a bit of life force or even to take a bit of telepathic energy. Courtney had worked with Stuart to enhance Stuart's basic shielding.

Someone in the clowder had to be very upset, angry, or sad,—it didn't matter—for anything to leak out and feed Chase. With that many people in the house, though, someone inevitably had a bad day.

Courtney, too, fed her entity from time to time. She ate

food like every day was a Thanksgiving feast just for her. As the clowder purchased food to prepare for a real Thanksgiving feast, Courtney worried about having enough to share with others. Despite her appetite, she was losing weight. The first ten pounds had felt good. The next ten had been okay. Now, she worried she'd fade away to nothing.

Her clothes hung on her. She'd been back to her little house once to get a bigger suitcase. She'd put wards around it to keep people from damaging anything. Someday, she'd have to go back. Or sell it. She fed on old loneliness while there, surprised that the entity hadn't already eaten it up. Then she'd understood that if it had eaten too much of her loneliness, she'd not have been able to face another day and she might have become seriously suicidal.

The entity hadn't been ready for her to die. It had needed her, at least at first.

It didn't need her now, but it was trapped while others worked to figure out how to get rid of it.

While Courtney had been at her house, her next door neighbor had come out, watching his truck. If he hadn't been out, she'd have worked to fix the smashed windows, but she couldn't do it with him watching. In theory, she knew she could erase his memory.

Courtney shuddered at the temptation of that ability. She could make people believe anything she wanted them to, forget anything she wanted them too. The entity lapped up her worries, but she was powerless to stop both the longing and the fears.

She'd talked to her parents, to her sister, to Hannah. She'd been good with Hannah, sipped from Payton while they spoke on the phone. With her father, she'd nearly broken the phone connection, she'd taken so much energy. Fortunately, she'd taken it from the connection and not purely from her father though a part of her wanted to let the entity loose on him.

Aware that such an action would make it harder to contain the entity, Courtney had rung off. There were things she wasn't going to be able to do. Talking much with her father was one of them.

Work was another. She hadn't even realized she'd been siphoning life force there until the third patient had fainted and had to be taken to the hospital. The doctors and nurses were concerned about something in the HVAC system and had started an investigation. In addition to fainting patients, other nurses, receptionists, and billers had been calling in sick. Just a vague malaise and fatigue.

Yesterday, Courtney had claimed to have it. She was looking into a leave of absence. It worried her to be without a paycheck. She needed to pay her mortgage. Stuart had assured her that while she was working with the clowder, they would take care of her.

That worry was moved to the back burner.

It left her only with the question of what she'd do next. If she couldn't trust herself around people, what would she do?

Courtney needed people, needed to be around them, always. She hated to be alone, but if she were taking life force from her coworkers because she was focused on doing her job, how could she ever again trust herself to work around people?

If she didn't know she'd scare everyone in the clowder, she'd scream in frustration and anger. She hadn't wanted this. Stuart seemed more interested in teaching her to use this power than in getting rid of the entity. Or maybe they were using her to get rid of Chase and they'd kill her after.

Maybe that was for the best. Maybe dying was the best thing she could do. Tears threatened. She didn't want to die. However, Courtney didn't see a future.

Not a future where her friends and family were safe.

Not with her in it.

The irony was that she had all this power, more power than anyone had ever seen. It was growing inside her as she took from the entity, as she learned to use it. Yet the only thing she could do would be to throw herself through the portal into a lifeless void. There had to be something else.

Smelling the turkey and ham and the fixings of the holiday, Courtney hugged a pillow close to her. They'd call her when it was dinner. Julia had laughed, sending her upstairs when Courtney offered to help. The last time Courtney had tried to cook, she'd eaten half the meal before it reached the table. The clowder wasn't taking that chance on Thanksgiving.

Courtney dipped into the life force of the clowder, just a bit, taking a bit of goodwill and cheer from each of them, savoring the flavors of their energies. She sipped from the telepathic bonds of the cats, but not so deeply as Chase had, she had no desire to cut them off from their bond-mates. It felt good to sip here and there.

Having taken that energy Courtney felt better. Stronger. More able to face whatever was coming, even if whatever was coming meant her death. She could face it. She realized as she had the thought that she knew the clowder would help her. Not because they had to, but because they thought of her as one of them, catless though she was.

It felt good to be part of a group that was so close, a group she could trust, at least as far as they were able, to keep the shadows and vampires at bay.

The final book in the Frost Witch Saga.

DECEMBER STORM

Most people would be overjoyed to see snow this close to Christmas, particularly in Central Kentucky where snow didn't fall often. Courtney sat on the too-soft sofa, sinking further down than she expected—something that happened no matter how often she plopped down—and looked at the tabletop Christmas tree without really seeing it. The second-floor room everyone called the library smelled of old books and cat urine.

Courtney tracked the falling white flakes as carefully as a hawk tracked a rat. The snow had started about an hour earlier and now fell quickly and silently through the gray sky. Her prediction on the arrival of the latest storm had been off by forty minutes.

From the room below, Courtney heard people talking, though she couldn't make out the words. She could have if she wanted to listen harder. The creature inside her wanted to reach out and feast on the emotions that were coming up. Worry and fear.

On the far side of the room, where Courtney was unable to see her, Riley worked her way through piles of books in hopes of finding a way to rid Courtney of the creature that tried to possess her. For now, Courtney had a hold on the thing and kept it at bay.

A calico cat curled beneath the little tree with its handful of ornaments. The oranges and blacks and whites and even a patch of gray on a hind foot were in stark contrast to the plain green tree skirt that covered the bookshelf upon which the cat and tree sat.

The bookshelf sat low beneath the big window. Full height shelves lined the walls between the windows, of which there were several. Shelves that came about chest height ran through the room. About midway, a large arch opened into the rest of the room. The arches offered more shelf space and likely helped carry the load of a weight-bearing wall. This was no ordinary home library.

Desks were tucked in here and there, though Courtney knew the household's researcher, Riley always took the one furthest back. While Courtney couldn't see Riley, the creature inside Courtney could smell her. All of Courtney's senses had been getting stronger but it was the sense of smell that continued to surprise her. She could smell when someone was happy or sad and she knew where every single woman was in her cycle with just a sniff.

The cats, all of whom weren't quite ordinary cats, had their own musky scents and Courtney knew which was which by now.

Anastasia, the calico cat sitting beneath the tree, moved into a crouch, waiting.

Something was outside. Courtney felt it suddenly, the thing inside her recoiling. Normally it wanted to reach out and feed. While the rest of the household still called it a frost witch, Courtney thought of her creature as a vampire. She'd never felt it recoil from anything before.

She stood up, intending to go downstairs. The floors

squeaked and groaned under Riley's ponderous walk as she hurried across the big room. Courtney waited, sensing, perhaps from the sounds, perhaps from the smells coming to her, that Riley wanted her to wait.

"Oh good, you're still here," Riley said.

Below, feet hurried to the door which squeaked gently as it opened.

"Why?" Courtney asked.

"It's the representative from Cat Home. Anastasia has word from Base Command that it would be best if you waited here." Riley watched her, perhaps hoping for some sign that Courtney understood.

Courtney hoped she gave nothing away. The creature inside her tried pushing at its cage, the bars of which Courtney had imagined into place, and Stuart, their Base Command representative, had helped solidify. It didn't like the Cat Home representative. If Courtney didn't know better, she'd have said the thing was afraid.

The feeling interested her. Until then, she wouldn't have said the frost witches had emotions. Normally they wanted to devour the energy of other people's emotions. Further, from everything Courtney knew, no one had encountered frost witches and survived so she didn't understand why the presence of any other creature would bother her frost witch.

Cat Home, of course, was the home world of the telepathic bond-mate cats, or so the stories went. The cats and those that created them dealt with the portals, something Courtney really didn't understand. She knew that most people didn't know about them and the creature inside her had come through one of them. She also knew that Cat Home had a different name but no one was able to pronounce it.

"Why?" Courtney asked Riley. The Cat Home representative clearly had nothing to fear from her or her passenger.

The frost witch waited, poised as if it were about to flee, though it had no place to go. The bars on the cage Courtney had created in her mind to keep the creature from possessing her held strong, at least for the moment.

"They need to get a feel for the house," Riley said. Her eyes went slightly unfocused. Courtney picked up a haze of static in her mind, the sense she had when the cats and their humans communicated telepathically.

"And they want to check out Chase first," Riley said. "Besides, with the snow today, no one is certain what will happen."

Courtney knew that. It's why she'd not been reading on her tablet, something she'd become accustomed to. She'd been restless all last night, the creature inside testing the cage walls, jumping at them. It had come to her then that it was going to snow and snow hard, soon.

She'd warned the others in the household, the clowder as they called themselves, and they'd closed the specially installed hurricane shutters. Matt had stayed on watch at the nearby portal, but Courtney knew, somehow, that the Cat Home representative had brought him back.

The temperature outside was dropping. Courtney felt it in her blood. She couldn't have described it better than that, only that she felt the coolness in the flow. The frost witches were on the ascendant.

Courtney wasn't sure if Cat Home had made the decision to send a representative here now because of the snow or if the snow was coming because of the representative. The two incidents were so intertwined that she didn't know how they'd unravel.

Sharp pain hit her beneath her ribs. Courtney drew in a breath. The pain felt icy cold. One of the bars of her prison had snapped. She closed her eyes, no longer worried about what Riley would pick up, and started focusing on rebuilding the bar. The frost witch hadn't done that before, hadn't been able to.

Whatever was going on had certainly given her creature a boost of power, something that hadn't happened in the month since Courtney had gained some control. On the edges of her consciousness, she heard Chase, her ex-boyfriend, who had his own frost witch, calling out, not just to her, but to someone else.

The witches had started causing trouble.

Before, they had started with mind games and manipulation. This time they were going directly for physical pain and, perhaps, injuries. Courtney wasn't sure if one was better than the other. Still, she was tired of the mind games, so she was thankful for that reprieve.

She stood up, still in pain but not nearly as much. Courtney had to get upstairs to her third floor room. She didn't feel ready to take on Chase or the representative from Cat Home, not when she was barely able to contain the thing inside her.

ABOUT BONNIE ELIZABETH

Bonnie Elizabeth could never decide what to do, so she wrote stories about amazing things and sometimes she even finished them.

While rejection stung her so badly in person, she spent most of her young life talking to cats and dogs rather than people, she was unusually resilient when it came to rejections on her writing, racking up a good number of them.

Floating through a variety of jobs, including veterinary receptionist, cemetery administrator, and finally acupuncturist, she continued to write stories.

When the internet came along (yes she's old), she started blogging as her cat, because we all know cats don't notice rejection. Then she started publishing.

Bonnie writes in a variety of genres. Her popular Whisper series is contemporary fantasy and her Teenage Fairy Godmother series is written for teens. She has been published in a number of anthologies and is working on expanding her writing repertoire.

She lives with her husband (who talks less than she does) and her three cats, who always talk back.

Stay in Touch

ALSO BY BONNIE ELIZABETH

THE FROST WITCH SAGA

October Snow

November Frost

December Storm

APPALACHIAN SOULS

Souls Lost

Souls Broken

THE ASH JERICHO SERIES

An Inheritance to Die For

A Discovery to Die For

A Distraction to Die For

THE WHISPER NOVELS

Whisper Bound

Taken by the Sound

An Air of Suspicion

Little Dog Lost

Death Interrupted

Down in Whisper

A Haunting Whisper

A Haunting Attraction

Secrets Not Whispers

Only Human

OTHER NOVELS

Ghosts from the Past

Unnatural Secrets

Find them all at your favorite bookseller or check us out at
MyBigFatOrangeCat.com